From Dawn 'Til Midnight

D.S. Edward

Hidden Message

FROM DAWN 'TIL MIDNIGHT

ISBN 978-0-9918423-2-2

FIRST EDITION

Inspired by true events

6:00 AM

      Dawn rolls over and switches on the lamp that sits atop the night stand. It's her first day back to work after a two week vacation, which means back to the morning routine. She pulls herself out of bed and, with half open eyes, finds her way to the kitchen, first to feed her year old tabby cat Cleopatra, and then to feed herself. Cleopatra – Cleo for short – greets Dawn in the kitchen with a series of mews. It's just the two of them, Dawn and Cleo, sharing the small, sparsely decorated, two bedroom apartment. The tidy white kitchen sits at one end of the main room, opposite the living room with its small sectional sofa, flat screen TV and computer. The only thing dividing the room is a line in the floor where the living room carpet ends and the kitchen tile begins.

Dawn pulls a bag of cat food out of the lower cabinet beside the stove and scoops some food into Cleo's dish. After filling the cat's water bowl, Dawn turns to pour herself a bowl of cereal. Gradually, she becomes more alert as she stands in the kitchen finishing her breakfast. Rinsing the bowl and laying it in the sink, she heads down the short hall to her bedroom where she lies on the floor for her morning stretches. There is plenty of floor space in the room, which only contains a few furnishings – a wrought-iron double bed, one night stand, and a small make-up table – no dresser – her clothes hang or rest neatly folded on shelves hidden behind two large, mirrored, closet doors.

Dawn's morning workout lasts about twenty minutes, give or take, and then she heads across the hall to the small, three piece bathroom for a shower. The shower spray completes her wake up process. Finally, fully alert she looks forward to the day. The day doesn't hold the same promise as she's become accustomed to over the last couple of weeks. The late August break that ends today, has been long and relaxing – a true vacation. She had taken two weeks off from both her full time job as an Office Administrator, and her part time modeling gig, and now today, it is back to work at both. After an eight hour day in the office, she will have her first photo shoot in more than three weeks. She doesn't mind the busy schedule though. Modeling, to Dawn, meant getting paid to have fun. As well, most days, Dawn enjoyed her work in the office. After ten years with the same company, she has found ways to overlook the negative and relish the positive. There is also the guilty pleasure that the two jobs afford her – dressing up – and dressing up has always been one of Dawn's greatest pleasures. She knows it is somewhat of a female stereotype, but she loves to shop. She loves looking for clothes, she loves purchasing clothes, and she loves the way she feels wearing that perfect ensemble that makes people notice.

It doesn't hurt that Dawn has the appearance to make any outfit look terrific. Simply stated, Dawn is beautiful – and turning thirty earlier this year hadn't hindered that fact at all. With long, black, naturally curly hair that flows just below half way down her back, and fair, porcelain skin, Dawn has often been compared to Snow White. And then there are her eyes – there was something about her eyes – piercing, bluish green and stunning. The small part of the Middle East in her heritage had produced invitingly mysterious eyes that frequently hypnotized both photographers and admirers alike. It isn't difficult to understand why so many are mesmerized by her beauty.

Dawn isn't tall, standing just five foot four, but the high heels that she loves to wear, brings her to five eight, and she strikes quite a statuesque pose. Not skinny, but slender, her body has curves that cause most men, and many women, to pause in admiration as Dawn walks by exuding confidence. Confidence that comes from years of trial and error – of figuring things out and getting things done – walking her own path and leading the way.

Dawn finishes her morning shower and sets to work on her hair, carefully working through the strands to manage the natural curl. With that task out of the way, she once again retreats to her bedroom and stands naked in front of the full length mirrors of her closet doors. Dawn's blown dry hair sits in a loose bun on her head as she applies her make-up. Not a lot of make-up – a little powder, some black eyeliner to highlight her eyes and some lip gloss – not lipstick – just a gloss to bring a shine to her already full red lips. Cleo plays behind Dawn on the bed, making a mess of the covers and begging for attention. Dinah Washington belts out her version of 'Love For Sale' from the stereo on the make-up table. Jazz is Dawn's music. Emotional, strong, intimate and often intensely sensual – or more to the point – sexual. Just like this song of a prostitute that Dawn is moving to as she performs her morning ritual leading up to choosing just the right clothes for the day.

Today Dawn has decided on an outfit that will emphasize her curves spectacularly, and accentuate her finer features. A tight fitting, black, pin stripe skirt that reaches down mid thigh. Directly in the center of the back is a slit that comes to a point just below the cheeks of her bottom. Dawn enjoys wearing skirts and showing off her legs. A skirt also means she won't bother with panties – and that is a feeling she loves. She is aware that the people at work wonder if she has anything on under her skirts. She can see the men straining to catch a view of a panty line that isn't there. If only they knew exactly what was hidden under the skirt, Dawn grins at the thought.

Dawn thinks that now, as she starts to pull on the skirt, and the thought causes her to move slowly and seductively in front of the mirror. Stopping with the top of her skirt half way up her thighs, Dawn runs her finger along her landing strip – a thin, neat line of hair about two and a half inches long that runs up from the tip of her 'pussy'. Dawn likes that word – 'pussy'. 'Vagina' is too cold and clinical. Other euphemisms seem ridiculous at their best and vulgar at their worst, but 'pussy' is soft and playful, which Dawn believes best describes that part of a woman's body.

As Dawn runs her finger along the strip, she remembers last night.

Unable to sleep – perhaps a little anxious about her return to work the next day – Dawn slips her hand under the sheets, finding that soft strip and running her finger along the length to the place where the strip and her pussy meet. Slowly, she allows her fingers to venture further searching for the release that will allow her to drift off to sleep. During these times, Dawn will turn to her 'purple rocket', a favorite and most convenient toy. The purple rocket is a small vibrator that applies just the right amount of stimuli to just the right spot – Dawn's clit.

Taking the rocket from it's hiding place under the bed, Dawn twists it, bringing it to life. Placing the tip to her clit, she closes her eyes and fades into a fantasy. It is frequently the same, simple fantasy – the touch of another person's fingers or tongue. And most often the other person that she envisions is a woman. There is no doubt of the pleasure that Dawn finds in the men of her life, but for some reason, in her fantasy world, it is the women that stand out. Dawn enjoys the gentle touch of a woman – and thinking of their kisses, their bodies, their touch, results in a speedy finish. It works again this time, her fantasy girl taking her to the edge and over the top, quickly bringing her the release she has been hoping for.

For a moment, the thoughts of last night tempt Dawn to find her purple rocket, but the reality of the day brings her back to the present, and she finishes pulling on her skirt, before reaching for a shirt. One of the great things about having smaller breasts is that she can wear extraordinarily open tops without being *all out there*. Dawn also loves the fact that a bra is not a necessity for her. And today Dawn has chosen to wear one of those exceptionally open tops – without a bra. Black, with a deep 'V' in front that crosses at her belly, the top opens to the edge of her firm, champagne glass breasts. The right move in any direction and the edge of her perfectly round aureola can be seen. As the thin material clings to her chest, Dawn realizes that the slightest bit of cool air shows off her erect nipples.

With her top in place, Dawn pulls the phone from her purse and calls the usual taxi company. She slips on her heels and pulls the elastic from her hair, letting her long curls fall out. Stuffing the phone back into it's place, she throws the handles of her purse over her shoulder, and grabs the bag that she's packed with clothes for changing into after work, stuffing her hairdryer inside. From the refrigerator, she snatches another bag containing the salad that she's prepared for her lunch. Taking one last look at her make-up, and blowing a kiss to Cleo, Dawn heads out the door to catch her cab.

7:20 AM

Dawn hates to drive, and public transit is too slow – cabs are pricey but convenient. As a bonus, every now and then Dawn will get a cab driver that is easy to talk to and genuinely kind. Today she meets just such a driver. Dawn quickly inspects the attractive driver, noticing his sharp brown eyes, square jaw and bright smile – and she can't help feeling that his features are somewhat familiar. Upon further inspection, Dawn notices the touches of white that spot the driver's neatly trimmed dark hair and she guesses him to be a little older than he first appeared – maybe fifty or so – regardless, the drivers apparent age only enhances his distinguished, good looks. As does his attire, his shirt and pants look casual but undeniably stylish – a little too stylish for a taxi driver. This is one cabbie that dresses to impress – and Dawn finds herself extremely impressed.

Dawn opens the taxi door, and the cabbie

greets her with a warm smile and friendly hello –
so warm and friendly that Dawn feels herself
blush. It distracts her for a moment as she climbs
into the back seat on the passenger side, and she
doesn't notice her top falling open a little. Not until
she looks up at the driver and follows the line of his
gaze, realizing that he's been provided with a full
view inside her shirt, but Dawn doesn't try to cover
up – instead she pretends she hasn't noticed, and
slowly takes her seat. The cabbie's eyes don't leave
Dawn's breast until her shirt closes, then almost
instantly the driver snaps out of his hypnotic state.
The cabbie raises his eyes and finds himself
staring straight into Dawn's eyes. He's been caught
– but as he scans Dawn's face he notices her
expression isn't one of anger or disapproval.
Instead he witnesses a warm and inviting smile,
followed by a relaxed, "Good morning."

As the cabbie struggles to keep eye contact
he asks, "Where are you headed?"

Dawn states her destination as she
reaches across her shoulder for the seat belt, all the
while planning her next move. The accidental flash,
and the cabbies accompanying response, has Dawn
feeling mischievous. What's wrong with a little
early morning fun? This time it won't be an
accidental flash, she thinks as she reaches for the
belt, purposely brushing her hand across her chest,
opening her top and fully exposing her right breast.
She leaves her shirt open as she leisurely buckles
her seat belt – hesitating before looking up to see
the cabbie's expression. His expression is blank –
his face frozen – his eyes fixed on the bare breast.
This is exactly the response that Dawn was hoping
for, and the sudden thrill gives her a chill

hardening her nipples instantly, which does not go unnoticed by the cabbie.

Nonchalantly, Dawn slowly closes her top, carefully watching the cabbie. And, as her breast disappears beneath her shirt, she once again catches his eyes as he looks up to meet her gaze with a smile.

With a wink and a grin, Dawn reminds the cabbie of the address, and she laughs to herself as he puts the cab in to gear. But before they drive off, Dawn observes the cabbie making a drastic adjustment to his rear view mirror, and it peaks her interest. Dawn becomes further intrigued as the cab ride continues in complete silence – no small talk – no chatter. She wonders if the friendly hello is the extent of the cabbie's vocabulary. Or was it the early morning exhibition that has left this cabbie speechless? Or maybe he feels the same as Dawn and is afraid that conversation will somehow destroy the sexual tension that has filled the cab. Something tells Dawn that the silence revolves around the cabbie's adjustment of the mirror and that he is simply waiting to see if the show will continue. If this is the case, Dawn decides, she likes the idea of playing along, and she comes up with a plan to test her theory.

Not wanting to distract the cabbie while they're moving, Dawn waits until the first stop light. As they come to a stop, Dawn feigns disinterest and stares out the side window, adjusting herself in the seat and spreading her legs slightly. Dawn listens for a reaction from the cabbie but hears nothing. She begins to think that she was all wrong about the situation until she observes the surrounding traffic moving forward while her taxi remains motionless. Quickly, Dawn turns to the cabbie and is pleasantly surprised to see the reflection in the rear view mirror showing a smile appearing on the cabbie's face, which confirms to Dawn exactly what the driver can see through the angled mirror. Dawn snaps her legs shut, causing the cabbie to regain focus, and immediately the taxi lurches forward playing catch up with the other morning commuters.

Dawn likes this game and contemplates her next move. Anticipating the next red light, she lifts her tight skirt as high as she can and waits for the right moment. Dawn's frustration begins to grow though, as the taxi cruises through intersection after intersection, managing to hit every green light. She smiles to herself when she notices the cabbie adjusting his speed, obviously trying to catch a red light, playing the game perfectly. With only a few intersections left, the tension rises in the taxi as both driver and passenger try to will the lights to change in their favor. And then finally, traffic slows as an amber light appears ahead. It is perfect timing for a long wait at a red light.

This is the last traffic light before work, and during the stop, Dawn wants to have as much fun as possible, so she lifts her skirt a little higher. She waits until the cab comes to a complete stop and she watches as the cabbie immediately turns his eyes to the mirror. Dawn spreads her legs wider. With her skirt already lifted to the top of her thighs, it raises even further as her thighs part. Dawn's legs spread – her skirt lifts – and looking down she sees her strip. She slides her bum forward a little on the seat – as far as the seat belt will allow – and spreads her legs as wide as possible, giving the cabbie a perfect view of her pussy. This is where she wants to be – this is what she wants the cabbie to see.

Dawn puts a hand in her shirt, pulling open the top to expose the breast that she's fondling. She reaches down with an index finger and runs her finger over her pussy, discovering that she is much wetter than she had thought. Looking up at the cabbie's eyes in the mirror, Dawn fingers her nipple and starts sliding her finger over her pussy. Just then, the sudden blast of a car horn startles her and she quickly sits up, closing her legs and looking around. Dawn notices the cabbie adjusting his mirror to look at the vehicles lined up behind them. The cabbie gives a polite smile and a nod, then pulls around the corner and into the first driveway. Dawn adjusts her skirt and straightens her top as the taxi drives toward the front of the building and the office entrance.

The parking lot is almost empty at this time of the morning. Dawn's plan was to get into work a little early to get settled back in after her vacation, and the empty lot reassures her that she is on time. The cab pulls into a spot away from the only other two cars that are already parked. Dawn grabs her bags and emerges from the back seat, closing the door behind her as the cabbie puts the front passenger side window down. Dawn muses over what to say, or if she should say anything, unsure of exactly what was going through the driver's mind. However, as Dawn leans in through the open window to pay the cabbie, she pauses noticing that his casual fitting pants are stretched tight by a large bulge. The cabbie's one hand sits in his lap, obviously trying to hide himself, to no avail, from Dawn's view. Dawn secretly applauds the cabbie's efforts, but that doesn't squelch her curiosity – she wants to see all that the driver is trying to cover up. Dawn holds out the money that she's taken from her purse, but not too far – and the cabbie is forced to reach, causing him to lift his hand off of his pants and grab the steering wheel to steady himself. And that's when Dawn notices the zipper on the cabbie's pants is open. The cabbie snaps the money out of Dawn's hand and attempts to recover – but it is too late. Dawn smiles at the driver as he looks down at his open pants and then back up to her with a sheepish grin, shrugging his shoulders. Dawn finds this somewhat amusing, but quite cute – the rugged, stylishly dressed cab driver and his shyness.

"Are you going to finish what you've started?" Dawn decides to ask.

The only response from the cabbie is an embarrassed and confused stare. Dawn scans the empty parking lot for possible intruders to their privacy. Assured that the coast is clear, she places her bags on the ground, and leans into the open window. Crossing her arms, she pulls on the sides of her shirt exposing both of her breasts. The cabbie's eyes widen as Dawn runs her forefingers over her hard nipples. Again, the cabbie looks down at himself and then up at her, starting to understand what Dawn is proposing. Dawn nods with an inviting smile enticing the cabbie to touch himself.

"Just do it," Dawn encourages.

With an expression of slight discomfort, the cabbie undoes his button and opens the front of his pants. Dawn bites her bottom lip in anticipation, looking at the slight wetness on the cabbie's white boxers. With one hand, the cabbie reaches into his boxers and grabs himself while using his other hand to pull down the front of his underwear. Dawn lets out a small gasp as she finally spies the cabbie's fully erect 'cock'. That's the word Dawn uses. Rarely, if ever, does she get poetic by using those terms that she's read in cheesy romance novels. When it's flaccid, it's a 'penis'. But when it is hard and throbbing, it is a 'cock'. And at this moment, Dawn is certainly enjoying the sight of the cabbie's cock. Her first thought is that it is longer than she expected, but then she realizes that she wasn't really sure what to expect. All she knows right now is that it is long, hard and beautiful.

Dawn's next thought is to wonder if the driver is as well groomed below as he is above, but all she can do is wonder, as the cabbie's shyness is preventing him from revealing more than the straight shaft that he is currently manhandling. She wishes that his pants were pulled lower or removed completely, and she almost finds the courage to request a more thorough view, but she quickly decides against the idea, not wanting to push too hard and disturb the timid presentation. So she silently watches as the cabbie holds his cock in his right hand and begins stroking himself – long, firm strokes as his eyes flash between Dawn's bare breasts and her face. Dawn urges him on with her stare and slight whispers of "yes".

As the driver begins to open his shirt buttons, Dawn can hear the quiet noises he's making – a mixture of sighs, moans and groans. The cabbie seems to be enjoying himself immensely, which thrills Dawn as her own whispers turn to gentle sighs. After releasing the final button, the cabbie pulls open his shirt showing off a toned torso. For a moment, he throws his head back and closes his eyes. As his sounds intensify, he looks to Dawn, searching her face for approval. Dawn doesn't notice the cabbie turning to stare at her once again – her eyes are fixed on his full cock and what he is doing to it.

Dawn sees the cabbie shudder a little – and then a little more – and she hears one long groan as the cum explodes from the head of his cock. It's a powerful orgasm that shoots cum all the way up the cabbie's bare chest, almost hitting him in the chin. The cabbie's breathing is heavy as he urges the cum from his cock with stroke after stroke. First spraying his chest, then his stomach, and then simply flowing over the head of his cock and down his fingers as he massages the tip releasing every last drop. Dawn breathes in deeply and smiles, and the cabbie smiles back, almost laughing. Dawn pulls her shirt back over her breasts and blows the cabbie a kiss.

"Very nice finish!" Dawn exclaims. "You're quite good at that."

The experience has left the cabbie dazed, and he murmurs the words, "Thank you."

"No – thank *you*," Dawn flirts. Before she can continue, she looks at the clock in the dash of the taxi and realizes, "I'm going to be late! Sorry – maybe we can do this again sometime."

Grabbing her bags, Dawn walks away feeling flush and excited, and tantalized by this new man that has suddenly appeared in her life. The taxi doesn't move until Dawn is about to enter the building, and then backs out and pulls away, just as Dawn realizes that she didn't get the driver's name. She turns back toward the parking lot, only to see the taxi driving off as cars begin to fill the empty parking spots.

"Maybe – sometime." Dawn tells herself.

7:55 AM

The door to the office is unlocked, and the lights are on when Dawn enters, telling her that she's not the first one to arrive. The sound of footsteps coming down the stairs from the upper office, confirms to Dawn that she is not alone. As the person enters the main floor office, Dawn recognizes that it is Derek, one of the new engineers. Derek has only been with the company for about three months, and Dawn doesn't know him very well. What Dawn does know is that Derek is around her age – and he's awkward – and he's cute. His hair is styled with a faux hawk, and he always wears a straight tie and long sleeved button up shirt. At first appearance, Derek is the type of guy that Dawn could find herself being attracted to, but that is where the attraction ends. The way Derek talks to Dawn and the way that he behaves around her makes him come off as a creepy, pervy high school boy, hardly ever looking Dawn in the eyes – today is no exception. The cold air from the office air conditioning hit Dawn the moment she entered, and she feels her nipples harden, attempting to force their way through the thin material of her shirt.

"Looks as if you enjoyed your vacation," remarks Derek with a smirk, pushing his slipping glasses back into place on his nose and staring directly at Dawn's protruding nipples.

What does that even mean? Dawn wonders as Derek continues, "Or is it just the long conversation you had with the cab driver that has you so perky this morning?"

There you go – creepy and pervy. Isn't that just like Derek. He must have been spying through his office window.

"Wow Derek," Dawn replies, "you can tell all that just from staring at my nipples?"

Derek's eyes quickly jump up to meet Dawn's.

"What?" he asks.

"Oh, and Derek, cover up. Everyone will be able to see your boner." Dawn walks toward the kitchen for her morning coffee, leaving Derek standing there with both hands crossed in front of his expanding pants, hiding his embarrassment.

First coffee – then check the email – then tackle the piles of paper that have accumulated on her desk during her absence – that is Dawn's plan. She hangs her bag of clothes in the closet near the back of the office, grabs the salad, and continues on her quest for a cup of coffee. Once in the kitchen, she places her salad in the fridge and pours her coffee. Dawn is greeted by a number of coworkers, all with the same questions, 'How was your vacation?' and 'Are you glad to be back?' She gives the same answers each time, "It was very relaxing." And, "I've enjoyed my day so far." Dawn hides her smile with a sip of coffee as she thinks of her cab ride to work and of the gorgeous cabbie – cock in hand and cum on his chest, and wonders again, maybe – sometime.

Then Derek walks in, indicating to Dawn that it is time to get to work. As she pushes past Derek, she takes a quick look down and states, "Your boner is still showing." She covers her laugh with another sip of coffee and leaves the kitchen. Again, Derek is left standing there – his hands crossed in front of him.

Dawn retreats to her desk, coffee in hand, ready for the official start of her day. Her desk is at the front of the office, by the large windows, which give her a perfect view of the outside world. A nice benefit to an otherwise typical work space. She places her coffee down and hides her purse away in her desk, before starting her computer and opening the email program. As two weeks of emails start pouring in, she switches on the radio beside her desk, filling the small space with the soft sounds of a local jazz station. Turning back to the computer screen, she clears the junk mail away, reducing the number of emails by more than half. However, that still leaves her with a good hour of reading and replying to the remaining messages.

Some of the emails are straightforward questions with quick, easy answers – Dawn replies to those first. Others are long and drawn out, and she scans through those ones, deciding which ones she will answer later, and which ones require her immediate attention. That's when she reads the subject line of an email from Marshal Preston, the president of the company – 'Take care of this'.

"Now what has he done?" Dawn says aloud.

Marshal Preston involved in any aspect of the company usually means trouble. A once prominent and respected man, he is now simply a figure head with extravagant taste, often putting a drain on company resources. The current success of the company can be attributed to the blood and sweat of those that are constantly cleaning up after him – and of course getting no respect from him in return. Too often, Dawn is given the task of watching over and dealing with the aftermath of Marshal Preston's latest idea. As Dawn opens the email, all she can think about is the mess that she will be responsible for dealing with.

Dawn

I tried to reach you on the weekend, but someone told me, you were still on vacation. I hope you're enjoying your holiday. I guess this can wait for Monday. I've hired a new employee in manufacturing. He is the son of my wife's friend. I'm actually not too fond of the boy, but my wife highly recommends him. The kid's name is David. He is almost 20, just finished 2 years of college, and has no prospects. I promised that I would hire this guy on for a short time to try and get him some experience. He was just hired last Friday, and today is his first day. Take care of the paperwork as soon as you can. I'll see you about this when I get in on Monday.

Marshal Preston
President & CEO
KPR E & M Inc.

This is so typical. Dawn knows that 'as soon as you can', means now. Usually Dawn would act right away on orders from Mr. Preston. It's either that or face another tantrum. Unfortunately, for Mr. Preston, this order would have to wait because Dawn views through the large windows that Sarah has just pulled up and is walking toward the front door.

Sarah works for one of KPR's biggest clients, and she stops by occasionally to check on the progress of certain projects. Over the years, Dawn and Sarah have become friendly, and Sarah's visits have become more frequent. Dawn follows Sarah's movements up the walkway. Her focus is on how beautiful Sarah looks with her long blonde hair and blue eyes. She's dressed in a business suit, with a tight skirt and high heels. The suit brags of confidence and hides Sarah's somewhat timid nature, but is a reflection of her position in the work force. Even though Dawn and Sarah have grown closer, Sarah has always seemed shyer around Dawn than around anyone else. That is the reason that Dawn had been so surprised as she talked to Sarah just before leaving for her vacation – she recalls Sarah opening up.

'I'll miss seeing you here.' Sarah had said to Dawn, three days before Dawn was to start her vacation. Dawn remembers how surprised she was at Sarah's admission, and her thoughts drift back to that day.

"I'll miss seeing you too."

"You could call me if you would like to get a drink or something."

"I could. Would you like me to?"

"I would." Sarah smiles – almost

blushing.

Dawn loves the thought of spending some time with Sarah, away from work. She had never told Sarah, but there were a number of sleepless nights when Sarah was the one that she had envisioned.

So Dawn calls her – by the fourth day of her vacation she knows she has to call. "I'm ready for that drink," Dawn says during the short phone conversation, and they arrange to get together on the patio at a restaurant near Dawn's apartment. Sarah agrees to meet Dawn after work – she just wants to go home to shower and change first.

Dawn gets to the restaurant around 5:30 in the afternoon, and makes her way past the diners inside, to the side door that opens up onto the patio. Her favorite spot is taken, but she is able to find a quiet table away from the crowd. She looks at herself in the window after ordering her first drink, and examines her reflection – the reflection of someone who is definitely on holiday. Flip-flops dangle from her feet – further up are a pair of tiny denim shorts – above those is an exceptionally loose top, hanging off one shoulder and tied up in the front, showing off her mid-drift. She looks over the top of her large sunglasses to get an untinted view of her complete vacation look, and she smirks at her reflection before returning her focus to her beverage.

She has moved on to her second drink when she spots Sarah walking up the sidewalk. The first thing that she notices is that Sarah has on a pair of shorts almost as small as her own. She then turns her eyes to the sleeveless, button up blouse, that Sarah is wearing – opened so low that the top half of Sarah's lacy bra can be seen. She also takes note of the high heels that Sarah has chosen. Together with the short shorts, the heels make Sarah's legs appear much longer than she had imagined. Dawn has seen Sarah in heels before, but never with so much leg revealed. Usually Sarah wears knee length skirts or slacks.

Seeing so much of Sarah for the first time gives Dawn a shiver. Or, Dawn thinks, maybe the shiver comes from the same light breeze that blows through Sarah's silky blonde hair. Dawn is slightly embarrassed at how taken she is by Sarah, as she finds herself staring and biting her lip while Sarah brushes the blown hair away from her face before entering the front door of the restaurant. Dawn watches through the window as Sarah finds her way through the restaurant and out onto the patio. Dawn stands and instinctively welcomes Sarah with a kiss on the cheek.

"Sorry if I've kept you waiting," Sarah apologizes. "I just had to put something on that is more suitable for the patio."

"I haven't been here long," Dawn replies. "Anyway, it was worth the wait; you look fantastic!"

Sarah shyly repays the compliment, "You look fantastic yourself."

Seeing the waitress approaching, Dawn asks Sarah, "Would you like something to eat?"

"A drink will be fine. What are you having?"

"Whiskey and club soda."

"Sounds good to me," Sarah says with a smile. And before Dawn can order Sarah instructs the waitress, "Two whiskey and club sodas please."

"Thank you."

There is mainly just small talk while they sip at the mixed drink, but the conversation begins to flow as easily as the drinks when the two start experimenting with a variety of cocktails on the menu. They talk a little about work while enjoying a couple of 'Slippery Nipples'. Then experience some 'Sex on the Beach' as Dawn shares stories of her modeling. They move on to the 'Wet Spot' during Sarah's tales of life outside of work – which consists mainly of sketching in the country, babysitting her two nephews and taking long bubble baths while reading a good book. Inevitably this leads them to try 'Between the Sheets' and a discussion of favorite books and authors. Then finally, an 'Orgasm' as they share their mutual interest in art.

The light is growing dim as the sun sets, and Sarah holds up her empty glass remarking, "I'm going to have to leave my car here tonight and call a taxi. I guess I'll just cab it back in the morning and pick it up."

"I only live a few blocks from here," Dawn replies. "We can walk there. You can stay the night if you'd like. It's a much shorter cab ride in the morning."

"Thanks Dawn, I was dreading having to get up early tomorrow."

The decision is made, and the two of them start their walk. They talk and laugh and lean on each other for balance as they make their way back to Dawn's apartment. Leaning turns to holding and by the time they enter the lobby of the building they are walking arm in arm. The laughs hush as they walk through the lobby and down the hall, and there is complete silence as the button is pushed summoning the elevator, and they wait. Both of them seem to have grown shyer, as they watch the descending numbers, willing the elevator to move faster.

Finally, the doors open and they enter the elevator. Dawn quickly pushes the eighth floor button and the doors close, locking them inside. The elevator moves, and so does Dawn – all evening she has held back. However, being alone in that small space, watching Sarah as she leans against the wall looking at the rising numbers and then back to her, is too much for Dawn's resistance. She closes the distance between them quickly, stares into Sarah's eyes, and kisses her. Dawn pulls back from the kiss and looks to Sarah for some approval. The approval comes when Sarah slowly leans in and kisses Dawn back. This kiss is deeper and longer, and neither one of them seems interested in seeing it come to an end, but they are stopped by the sound of the elevator doors opening on the eighth floor.

Without saying a word, they hold hands and jog down the hallway to the apartment. Everything is hurried at this point, and happening so fast. Key in door – door unlocked – door opened – enter – door closed – door locked. They kick off their shoes and Dawn pulls Sarah through the hall to the bedroom. Together they jump onto the bed, laughing at themselves and their mad rush.

Instantly, the hurry is over and they lay side by side, staring at each other. They stay like that for some time, eye to eye, as the laughter subsides. Then, as if timed, they both lean in, and they kiss. The kisses are soft, and they run their fingers across the other one's face, neck and body. Stroking backs, hips, thighs – each looking for whatever exposed skin may be available on the other.

Dawn works her hand over Sarah's hip and across her front. Coaxing Sarah's legs apart she slides her hand between them and gently massages Sarah's pussy through her shorts. Sarah holds her hand on Dawn's denim covered bum, squeezing in response to the massage her pussy is receiving. Slowly, Dawn moves toward the button of Sarah's shorts. She undoes the button, causing Sarah to shake. Then Dawn slides open the zipper and Sarah sighs, pushing against her.

Carefully, Dawn reaches her fingers into the shorts where she finds a small, soft patch of hair. Sarah pauses at that moment – waiting – wanting more. Dawn's fingers work their way down until they can feel the delicate surface of Sarah's pussy. She runs her forefinger along the outer edges a few times, wetting her finger, then moving it toward the center. Sliding her finger across smooth, wet softness Dawn finds Sarah's clit and makes that her focus.

Sarah's hips begin to move in motion to the clitoral massage, and she clumsily grabs at Dawn's shorts, finally getting the button open and the zipper unclasped. She pushes her hand into the open shorts finding Dawn's pussy, and quickly her middle finger enters Dawn, pleasantly startling them both. They move in unison, vocalizing their pleasure in the form of deep sighs and purring moans, while their legs spread wider, giving free reign to the hands and fingers.

Dawn moves her hand out of Sarah's shorts and up to the soft blouse that Sarah is wearing. Sarah's finger moves slower inside of Dawn as she watches Dawn unbutton the shirt and open the front. Sarah follows Dawn's lead and tugs at the knot on the front of Dawn's shirt until it gives way. Dawn lifts herself off of the bed and removes her own top before she goes after Sarah's blouse, pulling it open and sliding it off one arm at a time. In a singular fluid motion, Dawn drops Sarah's blouse to the floor, then slips her hand up Sarah's back, and releases the clasp from Sarah's bra.

Dawn lies Sarah onto her back and positions herself on top, straddling her mid section. Taking Sarah's bra straps in hand Dawn removes the bra as Sarah reaches up to touch the soft, supple flesh of Dawn's breasts. Dawn admiringly pauses for a moment as she looks upon Sarah's breasts for the first time. They are fabulous, she thinks – slightly larger than her own and topped with perfect pink nipples. Dawn grabs both of Sarah's breasts, one in each hand, and begins to finger Sarah's nipples while leaning forward and kissing her. They become engrossed in the kiss – tongues exploring mouths as hands explore breasts.

Dawn pulls her lips away from Sarah's and begins a progression of kisses and licks, starting at Sarah's neck and working down to her breasts. Once there Dawn kisses circles around one nipple before putting her mouth over it, licking and sucking. Then Dawn moves to the next breast, and it's delicate nipple, teasing it as she did the first. Back and forth, Dawn smothers Sarah's breasts and nipples with her kisses, before continuing the progression down Sarah's stomach.

Sarah can no longer reach Dawn's breasts and lets go, moving her hands to Dawn's shoulders and then to her head as Dawn moves further down. Dawn reaches the soft patch of hair and stops to play with it with her middle finger, before sliding the finger down across Sarah's clit and slipping it into her pussy. Sarah releases Dawn's head – forced to muffle her own loud exclamation with a hand. Sarah raises one hand to her mouth while running her other hand up and down her torso and over her breasts, occasionally pinching at each of her nipples.

Sarah's hips lift off of the bed as Dawn moves her finger around inside of her – and they don't lower until Dawn finally places her lips on her clit. Dawn's tongue flicks gently across Sarah's clit as she feels her swaying and pushing forward in response. Sarah's expressions of pleasure grow louder and Dawn knows that Sarah will orgasm soon. Which is exactly what she desires more than anything – to have Sarah climax from her touch. So she intensifies her attack on Sarah's clit and pussy – still gently, but with excited determination – pin-pointing those exact spots that seem to please Sarah the most.

Sarah's hips buck as she pushes her pussy against Dawn's mouth, and she lifts her head off of the pillow to look Dawn straight in the eyes. Pushed to the limit, Sarah's body shakes and then stiffens, again and again as Dawn presses for more, extending Sarah's orgasm to it's fullest. Finally, Sarah's head falls back onto the pillow as every muscle in her body relaxes. Dawn slips her finger out of Sarah's pussy slowly and touches her clit gently. With every movement of her finger, Dawn can feel Sarah shudder.

Carefully, Dawn kisses her way back up Sarah's body, eventually looking Sarah in the eyes and laying over her spread legs and out stretched body. Dawn presses her pelvis against Sarah's, eliciting a gentle moan from the still excited Sarah. Dawn repositions herself, raising her body and kneeling between Sarah's legs. Sarah sits up for a kiss as Dawn lifts her own legs over Sarah's hips, straddling Sarah's torso and pushing forward until their pussies meet. They kiss, and Sarah grabs Dawn's bum, holding her tightly, allowing her pussy to massage Dawn's clit as she moves her hips. In return, Dawn wraps her arms around Sarah and rubs her clit against Sarah's pussy.

The soft, wet flesh of Sarah's pussy nuzzled against Dawn's, causes an immediate and intense reaction from Dawn, and she pulls away from the kiss, moaning deeply as she throws her head back. Sarah covers Dawn's neck and breasts with kisses and nibbles, as she drives her hips toward Dawn. An orgasm begins to rise in Dawn's body and she pushes forward against Sarah, reciting a mantra of yeses. Reaching the apex of orgasm, Dawn buries her face in Sarah's shoulder, unsuccessfully attempting to muffle the rising screams.

Releasing their hold on each other, Dawn falls back onto the bed while Sarah collapses back onto the pillow. They lay like that, each of them gently massaging the other one's thighs – catching their breath before moving together to lie under the covers and drift off to sleep in an embrace.   Dawn and Sarah get together twice more during Dawn's vacation. One time they meet on the patio, before once again walking back to Dawn's apartment. This time they cut through the forest near Dawn's building, and Sarah chooses to take the initiative, holding Dawn up against a tree before sliding down her body and pleasuring her with soft kisses and licks.

The other time Sarah comes directly to Dawn's apartment. The door is barely closed when they begin making out. Never reaching the bedroom, they make love right there on the hallway floor.

"Welcome back."

Dawn is awakened from her daze. It's Sarah, and she is standing right in front of Dawn's desk.

"Need some help with that?" Sarah asks.

Dawn is confused by the question, still half in a trance from remembering her time with Sarah. She looks around the room – at her desk – at her computer – at Sarah – and again at her desk. And then Dawn looks at herself – her right hand to be exact. The hand that she presently notices is hidden under her skirt – and she quickly pulls the hand away.

"That's your fault," she says, looking at Sarah. "I didn't see you come in. How long have you been standing there?"

"Only a few minutes – or more," Sarah replies with a smile.

"I was just thinking that we should get together for a drink again – soon."

"A drink, eh?" Sarah smiles. "I'd like that." And she looks around.

Dawn stands up and looks around, as well. With no one in sight, Dawn leans over her desk and kisses Sarah gently on the lips. Sarah holds her eyes closed long after Dawn stops kissing her.

"Now who's daydreaming?" Dawn asks. "You're going to be late for your appointment."

Sarah blushes. She is there to meet with one of the engineers about a current project, and she is clearly late. With one more small kiss, Sarah heads for the upstairs offices, but before disappearing up the stairs, Sarah turns back to Dawn.

"Have fun at your photo shoot tonight," Sarah encourages – and then promises to pick up where they have left off.

9:05 AM

"Welcome back!"

Again, the same greeting, but this time it comes from Marshal Preston.

"Thank you," Dawn replies.

"How did things go with the new hire?"

"I'm just getting the paperwork together."

"I thought you would have had it done by now. I did say, 'as soon as you can'."

"I had to answer a number of emails!" Dawn can't hide the annoyance that is present in her voice, but proceeds calmly. "So, *soon* is, 'as soon as I can'."

"That's right," Marshal Preston continues, ignoring Dawn's responses and tone, "You've been on vacation. Welcome back! You probably have a number of emails to answer. Did you get to my email yet? Take care of that new hire as soon as you can."

And Marshal Preston walks away.

"I'll do that," Dawn responds, marvelling at Marshal Preston's oblivion and obvious ignorance as she searches the filing cabinet for the right forms.

Having found what she was looking for, Dawn heads out to the factory floor, and as soon as her heels hit the concrete, heads turn – and she laughs quietly, "No panty lines today guys."

For a moment, Dawn forgets the task that Marshal Preston has so emphatically pressed upon her. For now, she's just having fun with the attention – most of which comes from the men in the shop who see Dawn as an anomaly. Dawn is the 'person to turn to' at KPR – people depend on her when others fail. When the success of the company is discussed, Dawn's name is a positive part of the conversation. Dawn is that 'go to' person. At the same time, her beauty cannot be overlooked – so there is that stare – the struggle to see if Dawn has panty lines or not. The paradox excites Dawn, because she knows that she is the one to control the reaction. No one has ever considered crossing any line – unless she invites them.

Most of the men in the plant welcome Dawn back as she walks by, as do most of the women. Unfortunately, some of the women look at Dawn with disappointment. Disappointment that their hopes of Dawn suffering a tragic vacation accident have been dashed. And once again, Dawn laughs to herself.

Enough fun – Dawn returns her focus to the reason that she's on the shop floor. And that reason is David, the new hire. She marches to the back of the shop, searching for a new face. However, instead of a new face, she discovers a new figure at one of the work benches in the back. Dawn doesn't usually look to the shape of a man's body – she looks more to the face and eyes to find a connection, but the figure at the back of the shop draws her attention immediately. He's not overly muscular but certainly toned and defined – his broad shoulders hidden under a loose fitting black t-shirt that Dawn wishes were a slight bit tighter. The pants on the other hand, are plenty tight. Tight light colored jeans that cling to his bottom and hug his thighs. Dawn approaches the 'new hire'.

"David?" she asks.

David turns around with a start, "Hi!"

And there it is, in the eyes, the smile, the face – there is the connection, the attraction.

"Hello," Dawn responds.

They look at each other for what seems like several minutes before Dawn realizes that David is either too shy or too new to say more, and she should be the one to say something.

"You need to fill these out," she says, handing David the forms.

"Oh, okay."

"You can bring them into the office when you're done."

"Thank you."

And Dawn turns to walk away. She takes a few steps before turning back.

"I'm Dawn. If you can't find me, just ask someone."

David says nothing – just looks at her. Then finally, "I'm Dave."

"Fill out the forms and bring them to me in the office – Dave," Dawn says with a grin. And she walks away – only once looking back to see if David is still watching – he is.

9:25 AM

Dawn walks through the door to the office with a smile; courtesy of her brief encounter with David – maybe you did something right for a change Marshal Preston, she thinks. But her attention is quickly drawn away from the fantasy brewing in her mind when she spies the person who is standing by the photocopier. She instantly recognizes Carl, unsuccessfully attempting to make copies. Carl is one of the executives. That is to say, Carl is one of the key people that *actually* takes care of the company. A man who was hired to make sure Marshal Preston doesn't mess up the whole thing.

Carl is also one of Dawn's closest friends. They both started at KPR the same year. Ten years ago – Carl, already on his way to the top – Dawn, a temp. Carl took the time to befriend Dawn and help her find a permanent place in the company. Dawn, in turn, helped Carl through three promotions, and finally a place on the board. There had always been a sexual attraction between them, but that never played a part as their friendship grew.

Carl is the atypical tall, dark and handsome older gentleman. About fifteen years Dawn's senior, Carl always dresses well, is well spoken, kind, gentle – the perfect husband – which he is – to Beverly, another of Dawn's closest friends. Carl introduced Dawn to Beverly at the annual KPR company picnic nine years ago, and they hit it off immediately. After that, Carl and Beverly included Dawn in many of their private functions – including their wedding day – Dawn was a Bride's Maid. After that, there were family picnics, dinners out, trips to the theatre. Many times the three of them just sat and sipped tea while watching a movie at home. This is the way it had been for almost ten years. Until last year's Christmas party.

Marshal Preston likes to take care of his executives. And even though a majority of those executives don't think the same way as Preston, they play along to appease the man. See, to Marshal Preston it is always necessary to differentiate between the haves and the have-nots. Thus, the extravagant black town cars that he hires for the executives for every special KPR event. It is embarrassing for most of the executives, so they usually either leave early or stay late to avoid the awkward display of power.

Carl and Beverly are among the ones that will stay late. Long after Marshal

Preston drives off in his stretch limo, Carl and Beverly will continue to enjoy the evening, while also making sure everyone is taken care of and has a safe way home.

This year Dawn is one of the last ones out. Over the years, it has gradually become her responsibility that the party goes off without a hitch. So, after the last drink is consumed and the last hors d'oeuvres are devoured, Dawn stands in front of the restaurant in the blowing snow, pulling her long coat closed to keep out the wind, waiting for her cab. That's when the town car pulls up, and Beverly steps out of the back door on the driver's side.

"Let us give you a ride," she calls to Dawn.

"Thank you," Dawn replies, running through the deep snow. She meets Beverly at the open door, and Beverly motions for her to get in. Dawn jumps into the backseat where Carl is already sitting. Beverly pushes in behind Dawn and closes the door.

The interior is enormous. The big, bench seat reminds Dawn of a large, leather covered, plush sofa, and she sinks down into it as she sits. There is at least two feet of leg room between the front and back seats, and two small televisions are embedded in the back of the front seat. Between the televisions, a fold down tray contains assorted little bottles of alcohol and some glasses, all neatly tucked into their holders.

The driver looks over the back of

his seat. "Might as well get comfortable," he says, "the roads are really bad. It'll be slow going tonight."

"Well then," Beverly states, removing her coat and hanging it on the hook situated on the side of the car right behind the driver.

Dawn has always admired how elegant Beverly looks at all of the formal gatherings that they have attended together, but with the commotion and responsibility of the evening, she hasn't had the opportunity to really take in all of Beverly's elegance – until now.

Tonight, Beverly is wearing a long, black formal dress, with a slit going all of the way up her right leg revealing the top of her sheer black nylons. Dawn notices that the embroidery around the elastic is similar to that of her own nylons that she is wearing. She also notices that the top of Beverly's dress drapes over her shoulders and dips so low in the back that it is evident that wearing a bra with the dress would be impossible to conceal. However, the dress hangs loosely in the front, and it disguises the shape and size of Beverly's ample breasts.

Dawn keenly examines Beverly's more subtle qualities that are always present, but taken for granted. Beverly's long dark hair isn't naturally curly like Dawn's, but she spends hours with her hair in curlers to form ringlets that bounce off of her shoulders when she walks. She also takes tremendous care of her skin, and it pays off – she easily looks ten years younger than her actual age of forty-four.

Dawn looks over to Carl to see if he is also removing his coat, but he isn't wearing an overcoat tonight. Just a three piece black suit. He has removed his tie and unbuttoned the vest and top two buttons of his pressed white shirt.

Turning to Dawn, he offers, "Would you like me to help you with your coat?"

"Thank you," she replies and turns her back slightly toward Carl allowing him to hold the collar as she slips her arms out of the coat.

Dawn positions herself in her spot on the seat between Carl and Beverly and straightens the bottom of her short red halter style dress. Dawn had purchased the dress the previous summer, with this very night in mind. The dress is tied in two places with thin spaghetti straps. One set of straps ties behind her neck holding in place the two pieces of material that cover her breasts. The other set ties in the back around her waist. The front is open in a 'V' that goes as far down as her bellybutton, and her back is entirely bare from the waist up. The lower part of the dress is made up of layers of thin material that hang unevenly at the bottom, showing off the tops of her black nylons.

Both of the ladies kick off their shoes as Carl looks through the darkly tinted window at the blizzard going on outside. The driver is playing a Dean

Martin Christmas CD – one of Dawn's favorites. And they all sit in silence, listening to the soft voice of the crooner as the car inches along through the snow covered streets.

Maybe it is too silent for Beverly, or maybe it is because of the glasses of champagne she consumed at the party – whatever it is that prompts her to speak up, Beverly's words make Dawn blush slightly.

"I don't understand Carl," Beverly muses. "Working for ten years in the same office as this beautiful young woman, and not once have you hit on her."

Carl laughs, "It's not like I haven't thought about it." And he continues to stare out the window.

"Have you ever even asked her for a kiss?" Beverly prods.

Carl attempts to hide the discomfort brought on by this line of questioning by focusing on the snow flying outside the car window. "No, not even so much as a peck on the cheek."

"But you've thought about it?"

Carl turns and looks at Beverly. "What are you getting at Beverly?"

"I think you should ask," Beverly continues. "The worst thing that could happen is that she might say no."

Dawn squirms in her seat, feeling a little awkward as the two talk around her. Unsure of who to look at, she stares at her shoes lying on the floor at her feet.

Carl smugly laughs, "Fine." Then

he looks at Dawn. "Dawn, may I have a kiss?"

Little do they know that Dawn has thought many times of kissing Carl – and more, but she has so much love for Carl and Beverly, and respect for their marriage, she has never considered pursuing Carl in a sexual manner. Even though it is Carl that asked the question, Dawn looks to Beverly. As she does, she detects a smile, followed by a nod of approval. That is all the assurance that Dawn needs to pursue her little fantasy.

She turns to Carl and blurts out with a smile, "Sure!"

Not wanting to appear over eager, Dawn waits for Carl to move. They look into each other's eyes for a moment and then Carl leans in. Their lips meet in a quick gentle kiss. Dawn waits to see if there will be more as she continues to allow Carl to take the lead. And then comes a second quick kiss. The pause is much shorter after the second kiss, and as their lips touch for a third time, Dawn opens her mouth slightly and licks Carl's lower lip. Switching lip position, Carl gently nibbles on Dawn's lower lip. Finally, both of them open their mouths and press together. Their tongues meet, and they kiss passionately.

Dawn wonders how far Beverly and Carl are going to take things, as Carl places his hand on the side of her cheek. It's at this moment that Dawn feels Beverly's hand fall to rest on top of her left thigh. She pulls back from the kiss looking into Carl's eyes one more time before turning to Beverly.

"Dawn?" Beverly asks. "May I..."

Desiring to explore where this situation is headed, and already aroused by Carl's kiss, Dawn doesn't wait for Beverly to finish her question. She leans toward Beverly and begins excitedly kissing her, taking up where she had left off with Carl. Dawn feels Carl's hand move over onto her right thigh, still feeling Beverly's hand on her left. Dawn's hands remain beside her, pushing down on the seat as if to hold herself up. Beverly uses her free hand to reach under Dawn's hair and untie the strap holding the upper part of Dawn's dress in place. As the tie lets loose, Dawn's dress falls. She stops kissing Beverly and looks down at herself and her exposed breasts.

Just then Dawn thinks of the driver and looks up to see if he may be watching. She only sees his brown eyes in the rear view mirror, but they are watching the road, not the backseat. Dawn wonders if the driver has glanced back at all, and the thought of it makes her tingle, causing her nipples to harden. Then, as if on cue, the driver's eyes move in the mirror and catch Dawn staring. Dawn looks straight into the reflection of the driver's smiling eyes as she feels Carl and Beverly's mouths on her neck, and she closes her eyes, laying her head back. Dawn stiffens as her hosts kiss their way down to her breasts. Carl makes it to her right breast first, circling his tongue around her nipple. Then taking the nipple into his mouth just as Beverly finds Dawn's left breast with her lips.

Almost simultaneously, Carl lifts Dawn's right leg onto his lap as Beverly lifts Dawn's left leg onto her lap. Her legs spread wide, Dawn feels the hands of the couple moving up her thighs and under her dress. This time it is Beverly that makes it to the spot first, but Carl is also there, almost immediately after. Carl and Beverly pause for a moment, looking at each other as they discover Dawn's uncovered and wet pussy – dresses, like skirts, means no panties.

Carl and Beverly are both surprisingly gentle as they massage Dawn's pussy with their fingers. They begin taking turns – one plays with her clit while the other slides a finger in and out of her. And then they switch. Back and forth they trade off, the whole time continuing to give specific attention to Dawn's breasts with their mouths.

Dawn desires to repay the pleasure she is receiving, and she lifts her hands off of the seat. With her left hand, she finds her way through the slit in Beverly's dress, and with her right hand she begins working at the clasp and zipper on Carl's pants. Beverly doesn't hold to the same 'no panties' policy that Dawn does, so Dawn slides her hand down the front of Beverly's lace panties until she finds her pussy. Beverly is already moist, which makes it easy for Dawn to slide her finger over Beverly's clit and into her pussy. Dawn repeats the same motion over and over making sure to pleasure Beverly's clit with a few turns of her finger before slipping it back inside her pussy.

All the while, Dawn has been working at Carl. She has already opened his pants – pushed aside his boxers – and now holds his stiff cock in her hand. With her eyes still closed, she can feel that Carl is of average size in length but quite large in girth. She strokes his cock firmly, occasionally running her finger across the slick tip.

Dawn's hands are in full motion as she feels herself on the brink of orgasm. She begins lifting her bum off of the seat and pressing her pussy against the probing fingers of the enthusiastic couple. The sounds coming from Dawn's throat grow louder, and she opens her mouth to let them out. She doesn't care where she is or who is listening – this feels wonderful, and she *is* cumming. She calls out their names, "Carl! – Beverly!" And repeats over and over again, "Yes!" As her climax peaks, forcing her hips high in the air.

Completely engrossed in the passion of the moment, Dawn pulls away from the mouths on her breasts and the fingers on her pussy. She leans over towards Carl, not for a kiss, but to take his cock into her mouth. Carl gasps as Dawn runs her tongue from the base to the tip and then passes the head of his cock through her lips, and to the back of her throat. Stroking the shaft with one hand, Dawn licks around the head of Carl's swollen cock, flicking her tongue on the tip and then again takes him into her mouth.

Beverly lifts Dawn's left leg onto the seat and positions herself between her legs. She sits on the floor of the car and presses her lips against Dawn's pussy. Sucking and licking Dawn's clit and pussy, Beverly looks over to watch Dawn enjoy Carl's cock. Carl sits there, the pleasure forcing him to throw his head back, but the sight of Dawn sucking his cock pulls him forward again to watch. He looks over at Beverly, delighting in what he is witnessing his wife doing to Dawn. The experience is overwhelming for Carl, and he can feel himself quickly edging toward orgasm.

Dawn notices this and decides to reposition her body. She lets go of Carl's cock and guides Beverly away from her pussy. Then she motions for Beverly to sit on the seat with her back toward the side of the car. Dawn reaches under Beverly's dress and pulls down her delicate panties. There is a pause as Dawn enjoys her first view of Beverly and her neatly trimmed 'V' of dark hair. Below the 'V' is a completely shaved and extremely wet pussy.

Dawn catches Beverly's eyes with her own. Still looking directly at each other, Dawn lowers her mouth to Beverly's pussy, first sliding her tongue inside of her, and then focusing on the clit. Beverly closes her eyes and breathes in deeply as Dawn slips a finger inside her pussy, all the while, tickling her clit with her tongue.

Carl is frozen, and he sits admiring his wife and exalting in the pleasure Dawn is giving her. Dawn is on her knees on the edge of the seat, and Carl has a perfect view of her incredible bum and glistening pussy. He discovers quickly that this isn't accidental as Dawn sways her hips back and forth, offering herself to him. Dawn slides her free hand between her legs and brushes her middle finger up and down over her pussy, letting it slide into herself occasionally.

The hint is received and Carl pulls off his pants and boxers, positioning himself behind Dawn. Dawn reaches further between her legs and grabs hold of Carl's approaching cock. Again she feels the girth, and it startles her, but she wants him inside of her. Dawn guides Carl to her pussy and rubs the head against herself, covering it with her wetness. Then holding Carl's balls, Dawn leads him into her.

Beverly watches the look on her husband's face as his cock enters Dawn, and the sight makes her even more responsive to Dawn's fingers and tongue. Carl, realizing how tight Dawn is against the width of his cock, takes care not to be too forceful. A little at a time he slides in and then pulls back, each time moving deeper into Dawn with every forward motion. The sensation overtakes Dawn and she moans with pleasure, intensifying her stimulation of Beverly's pussy. Carl, feeling Dawn fully open and receiving his cock, begins to quicken his pace. Beverly is eager to cum and pushes against Dawn's mouth. Dawn can feel herself getting to that point again as she takes Carl all of the way inside. Carl holds Dawn's hips and moves in time with her as she satisfies his wife – he is close to exploding and stutters through tight lips, "I'm cumming!" And he starts to pull out.

"Don't stop!" Dawn cries and reaches around grabbing Carl's bum, holding him inside her.

"Cum inside her!" Beverly begs Carl.

Carl pushes back inside Dawn – deeper than before – and Dawn reacts, her mouth opening wide with a silent scream of pleasure. Beverly's scream isn't so silent as her orgasm begins. Dawn pushes her mouth against Beverly's pussy and her own pussy against Carl's cock. Beverly starts the chain reaction. She lifts her hips again and again, bucking against Dawn's mouth and fingers as she cums. This pushes Carl to the edge and he drives deep inside of Dawn, filling her pussy with his cum. Dawn can take no more, feeling Carl's warm stream in her depths and hearing Beverly's screams of delight. Dawn cums again – this time even harder than before.

Dawn melts into Beverly's arms. Carl collapses to the floor beside the two ladies. The three of them touch, kiss and gently caress each other as they lay there catching their breath before reaching for their clothes.

As if recognizing that the events in the backseat are concluded, the driver announces, "We're approaching your home. Will I be dropping the young lady off with you or continuing on, to take her home?"

Beverly looks to Dawn, and asks as they get dressed, "Would you like to stay the night with us?"

Dawn has spent a number of nights at Carl and Beverly's home. Usually after a late night of watching movies in their basement screening room. The guest room that she always stays in is equipped with all of the comforts of home, including a private bathroom, and an invitation to stay is always welcome.

"That would be great," Dawn replies.

A short time later, the car pulls into the driveway of Carl and Beverly's luxury home. Carl leans forward and hands the driver two, new hundred dollar bills. The driver smiles and takes the money from Carl, and the two of them start chatting. Dawn watches the two men as they converse and wonders how much the driver has seen of what has gone on in the back of his car. Dawn can't hear what they are saying and suddenly feels shy thinking that maybe they *are* talking about the evening's events in the backseat. Whatever they are discussing, at one point Dawn catches the driver's eye. They smile at each other — only briefly — but it is enough to make Dawn blush – and it appears that the driver is blushing a little, as well.

Carl opens the door and helps Dawn and Beverly out of the backseat. The three of them walk up to the house and enter as the town car drives off into the snowy night. Once inside, they hang up their coats and Dawn turns to head toward the guest room. Beverly stops her.

"You don't have to use the guest room tonight," she says. "You're welcome to come upstairs with us. We could grab a hot shower, and Carl can build a fire in the fireplace."

Dawn smiles and thanks Beverly, and the trio head upstairs to the master suite. Dawn has never seen this room before and is amazed at the size and opulence. Extending from the near wall, is a solid oak, king size canopy bed, complete with a mattress so high in stature that it looks as if you would need a ladder to get on top. Across from the bed, on the other side of the expansive room, two loveseats sit facing each other in front of a beautiful stone fireplace. Extravagant french doors line the wall to the left of the bed, allowing a view of a grand terrace. To the right of the bed are two large walk-in closets, divided by a hallway that leads to the en suite bathroom.

"You two go ahead and get in the shower," Carl says. "I'll start a fire and join you in a minute."

Beverly leads Dawn to the en suite. The washroom is fabulous, with two marble sinks, a toilet with accompanying bidet, a large whirlpool tub suitable for four persons, and an enormous glass enclosed shower with five shower heads.

Beverly turns the valve in the shower and warm water comes spraying out of all five shower heads. Beverly and Dawn undress and step inside. This is Dawn's first look at Beverly fully naked, and her eyes follow the water as it flows over Beverly's large breasts, snaking it's way around the curves of her body.

Through the glass, Dawn can see Carl is already naked as he enters the washroom. It is obvious to her that he takes extremely good care of his body – muscular but not bulky. As Carl walks toward the shower, Dawn notices a neatly trimmed 'V', similar to Beverly's, pointing toward a penis that has lost some of its girth, but none of its appeal, in its soft state. Below that, Carl's balls look as soft and smooth as they had felt to Dawn in the limo. While Carl turns to close the door behind himself as he enters the shower, Dawn gets a perfect look at Carl's gorgeous bum, and she struggles to resist the urge to reach out with both hands and squeeze. Eventually giving into the urge, she playfully gives Carl's cheeks a squeeze and a slap, bringing about laughter that echoes off of the ceramic walls.

Dawn loves being naked in the shower with both Carl and Beverly. The couple begin to wash Dawn using puffs and their hands, admiring and exploring every inch of her body. Dawn, in turn, washes each of them in the same admiring and exploring manner. Their deep friendship is obviously adding to the experience, and they chat leisurely as their hands move about each other's wet bodies. An hour goes by before Beverly finally shuts off the water, and the three of them get out of the shower. Beverly pulls a towel from the rack as Carl takes two towels from the same rack, offering one to Dawn. While they dry themselves off, Dawn watches as Carl attempts to hide an erection behind his towel. The shower seems to have brought Carl back to life, and Dawn flashes him a flirtatious smile of approval.

Beverly notices the interaction and comments, "I can't believe that you two waited ten years for this."

"Why did you wait?" Dawn responds.

"Yeah," Carl adds. "Why did you wait?"

"I was just waiting for the perfect moment," comes Beverly's answer.

"Well, you seem to have found the perfect moment," Dawn jokes.

"It was pretty perfect, wasn't it?" Beverly chides. "Now maybe you two can relax and enjoy yourselves in the future."

Carl walks up to Beverly and kisses her, then comments, "You set me up."

"I set us both up."

"You're bad."

Beverly motions for Dawn to join

in the embrace, and the three of them stand there sharing a hug and kisses before leaving the washroom to retire to the bedroom. The fire is burning brightly in the fireplace, providing the only light in the room as they move to the bed. Carl and Beverly shed their towels and climb under the covers on opposite sides of the enormous bed. Dawn nestles down naked between the couple, feeling the heat from their nude bodies. Exhausted from the evening's events, she thinks of how warm and cozy this feels as she drifts off to sleep.

Some time during the early morning hours Dawn is awakened by sounds and movement in the bed. The fire has died down, and there is only a soft glow from the embers. She looks toward Beverly who is now laying on her side facing away from Dawn, sleeping soundly. Dawn thinks that perhaps Carl is snoring and that could have been the sound that woke her. She listens and realizes the sounds are coming from Carl, but it isn't snoring she hears – just heavy breathing and quiet sighs. The movement that accompanies the sounds is coming from under the blankets, on Carl's side of the bed. Suddenly it occurs to Dawn – Carl is masturbating!

"Carl?" she whispers.

Carl stops his activity, startled by Dawn's voice.

"Sorry. Did I wake you?" he replies softly.

"Are you jerking off?"

"Sorry. I woke up still thinking of everything that went on tonight. I couldn't help myself."

"I don't mind," Dawn remarks in her hushed voice. "You don't have to stop."

Carl looks at Dawn in the dim light and then over at the still body of his sleeping wife. Remembering Beverly's approval and encouragement, he hesitantly resumes stroking his stiffening cock. Even with Beverly's blessing, Dawn senses Carl's nervousness at this quiet moment between the two of them. She moves closer to Carl and presses her lips to his, evoking a kiss. With her finger, she starts tracing circles on his chest and around his nipples. Carl responds with heavier breathing and faster strokes. Dawn's lips find their way down to Carl's nipples and she begins licking and sucking each of them. Again Carl responds, breathing heavier still.

"I'm almost there," he inhales deeply.

Dawn reaches under the covers and grabs Carl's hand, stopping the rhythmic pumping. Carl looks at Dawn, not sure why she has stopped him.

"You're teasing me Dawn," Carl whimpers.

Dawn smiles and pulls Carl's hand away from his cock, replacing it with her own hand.

"You don't want to make a mess of these expensive sheets," Dawn flirts.

Carl looks confused.

"But..." he mutters.

Dawn doesn't let him finish his complaint. She slowly slips under the covers. Carl looks down as Dawn disappears beneath the sheets. Then he looks up at the ceiling and gasps, "Oh god!" as he feels Dawn's mouth slide over the head of his cock. He watches the covers move up and down as Dawn sucks his cock, taking it in as far as she can, then pulling back until just the head is in her mouth. Repeating the motion over and over, sliding her tongue up and down the length of Carl's cock as she moves. Carl can hear Dawn's moans as she proceeds, apparently enjoying what she is doing. That is too much for Carl, and he warns Dawn that he is ready to cum, only to hear a delighted moan from Dawn's occupied lips.

The first blast of cum is enough to fill Dawn's mouth, and she has to swallow quick to make room for more – and there is more. Again and again Carl's cock throbs and streams of cum shoot from the head. Dawn swallows a second time before the flow of thick liquid finally slows. She continues to suck on the head of Carl's cock, drawing out every last drop of cum, and then swallowing once more.

Emerging from under the covers, Dawn smiles as she looks at Carl's contented expression. She stretches out and lays on top of Carl, and the two of them kiss and laugh quietly together before Dawn moves back to her position in the middle of the bed. Beverly, still fast asleep, has not moved a muscle. Dawn once again sinks into the warm and cozy feeling, blissfully drifting off to sleep.

Dawn awakes hours later, alone amongst the sheets of the oversized bed, the smell of bacon and coffee wafting through the room. She throws on the robe that has been laid out at the foot of the bed, and finds her way downstairs. Following the sounds of casual conversation, Dawn meets Carl and Beverly in the kitchen. Beverly greets Dawn with a kiss while Carl leans against the counter, staring into his cup of coffee. It quickly becomes apparent to Dawn that the casual conversation that drew her into the kitchen was about the quiet moment that Carl and her had shared during the night. So, the three of them discuss the early morning adventure over breakfast.

Carl paints a vivid picture of the event for Beverly, amusing and exciting her to the point that she taunts and begs for an immediate re-enactment. The taunting, is having a recognizable effect on Carl, and Dawn spies Carl's stiffening cock poking through the front of his bathrobe. Playfully, Dawn opens her robe and approaches Carl. She decides that she is more than willing to play out the event for Beverly and she drops to her knees for her friend.

As Dawn kneels down before Carl, she takes hold of the stiffness protruding through the gap in his robe, and proceeds to give him a rather dramatic blow job right there in the kitchen, putting on her best show for Beverly, who is eagerly looking on. This time Dawn chooses to pull Carl out of her mouth at the last moment, and Beverly thrills at the site of Carl covering Dawn's neck and breasts with cum. With one hand, Dawn coaxes every drop from Carl, and with the other hand she enticingly distributes the cum over her breasts, amazed at the amount that Carl was able to produce after such an active night. Jokingly Beverly applauds, and laughs at the shocked look on Carl's face.

Dawn laughs to herself remembering the look on Carl's face that morning. The friendship between Dawn and the couple remained strong after that first encounter, and in many ways grew stronger. Together, they still did the usual things, like picnics, theatre, and sipping tea together. But every now and then they would throw more playful moments into the mix. Usually it would be the three of them together. But some times it was just Dawn and Beverly alone, or with Carl sitting nearby with a glass of cognac, taking in the view of the two beautiful women making love. And occasionally it was just Dawn, dropping to her knees and giving Carl a surprise.

I should drop and give him one right now, Dawn thinks as she approaches Carl at the photocopier.

"Welcome back Dawn!" Carl exclaims. He turns his attention away from his frustration with the photocopier. "We've missed you around here."

"Thanks Carl," Dawn smiles.

They both look around to be sure they are alone, before sharing a hug and a kiss.

"I wish Beverly and I would have had some time to get together with you while you were on vacation," Carl comments. "But with you not here, I've been working late to stay on top of things. I don't know what we'd do without you if you were ever gone for more than two weeks."

"Thank you," Dawn humbly acknowledges the compliment. "The three of us should get together this weekend. It's been too long. I miss Beverly. And it's been a while since I've given you a surprise."

The comment keeps Carl grinning broadly as he watches Dawn rearrange the clumsy pile of papers in the photocopier, adjust a couple of settings and hit the 'Start' button. The copier comes to life. And Dawn walks away with a smirk.

"What would we do without you?" Carl smiles and shakes his head, before retrieving his papers from the machine. He turns to walk away and hears Dawn's voice.

"Don't forget the originals, Carl."

Carl turns back to the copier and removes the originals from the top, shaking his head and laughing at himself.

11:56 AM

It's almost noon and Dawn has spent the rest of her morning answering the remaining emails and catching up on 'Project Analysis' reports. Wanting to get through the backlog of paperwork as soon as possible, so that she can leave early to enjoy a quiet dinner after work before heading to her photo shoot, Dawn chooses to eat lunch at her desk. Removing the lid from the salad that she has retrieved from the fridge, she reaches over and turns up the radio. Working through lunch requires a little extra motivation, and between bites of salad, she loudly sings along to Billy Holiday's 'Don't Explain' as she works.

Dawn pushes through the individual stacks of paper, knocking off one task after the other – employee time sheets, accounts receivable, accounts payable – everything being entered into it's proper place in the database. Finished her lunch, she starts to attack the pile of purchase orders. Each one must be photocopied and placed in the proper binder or folder. She carries the pile of papers to the copier and places them in the upper tray. Then, as she's done hundreds of times before, she adjusts a couple of settings and hits the 'Start' button, and – nothing – nothing except a flashing message on the screen, 'Paper Tray Empty'. Don't forget to refill the paper if you use it all Carl, she thinks with a smile, before heading to retrieve more paper.

The copier paper is kept in a locked cabinet in the boardroom. Why the cabinet is locked and why in the boardroom, Dawn never understood. Other than the fact that Marshal Preston treated paper like gold and monitored it's use carefully. She grabs the key out of her desk drawer and enters the boardroom door that is situated directly across from her desk. Turning on the light, she makes her way to the cabinet.

The room is windowless, large and sparsely furnished. A long, oval table surrounded by leather chairs sits in the middle of the room. In one corner is a display case, showing off KPR's latest innovations. In another corner is a big screen television, set up for presentations. Against the end wall stands a board covered in nonsensical writing that the department heads use to impress their staff. The cabinet that Dawn is looking for sits against the opposite wall of the doorway.

Dawn crosses the room and unlocks the cabinet. The paper she needs is on the very bottom shelf. The tight skirt she's wearing, while fashionable and sexy, makes performing basic tasks, such as squatting, nearly impossible. So she bends at the waist, even though she knows that her skirt will lift in the back and the slit in the center will open up. This isn't normally a problem, when it's a quick motion of bending over and picking something up, but the box of paper is sealed, and she struggles with the bands holding the box shut, leaving herself exposed for longer than anticipated.

Dawn's feeling of exposure increases, as the task drags on for much too long. Making her feel even more exposed is a sensation of being watched – a discernment that she is not alone. And then comes the sudden awareness that someone is silently standing in the doorway. It has to be Derek, she thinks, and she turns quickly, ready to confront him. Only it's not Derek – it's David. His eyes are open wide, and his mouth appears frozen half sentence.

"Looking for something, David?" Dawn asks.

"I'm sorry," he replies. "I didn't know what to say."

"How about, 'Hello Dawn', or maybe a knock on the door – something to announce your presence!"

David is caught off guard by Dawn's abrupt response.

"I – should have," he stutters. "I'm really sorry – I mean I apologize – it's not that I'm sorry I saw – I liked it – I like it – I mean what I saw – but – I should have said something."

David stares awkwardly at Dawn for a moment while her eyes bore holes in him as she stares back intently.

"I have the forms – and I'm bringing them to you like you asked," David attempts to explain.

Dawn is unable to hold her stare, amused by David's apology/explanation, and she finds that the initial attraction that she felt in the shop is growing more intense. David obviously did have a good view of her, and the thought elevates her arousal in equal measure to her attraction as she pictures him standing in the doorway, sneaking a peak at her pussy. And she thinks, that this couldn't be better if she had planned it.

"Don't worry," she says with a reassuring grin. "Come on in and close the door. Grab a seat."

David does as he's told, closing the door, before sitting in one of the leather chairs. Dawn sits close to David, on the edge of the large, oval table, taking the forms that he is offering her. As Dawn reads over the forms, her eyes drift from the pages to David. He seems to look more at her skirt than anything else in the room – at times, awkwardly staring.

"Well," Dawn announces as she shifts her position slightly.

David looks up at Dawn, waiting for her to continue. When Dawn doesn't immediately finish her sentence, David's gaze drifts back to her skirt. However, David is now seeing more than he was seeing before. Dawn has parted her legs just enough to allow David a glimpse of something more. He doesn't have a good enough view to see everything, but enough of a view to see Dawn's white thighs fade into the shadow under her skirt. Dawn watches as David swallows hard and tilts his head a little to one side in an attempt to see deeper into the shadow.

"It looks like you filled out all of the forms correctly," Dawn finally continues.

David doesn't care about the forms anymore. His mind is occupied with less formal things, and he looks up at Dawn

"So, you're really not upset with me?" he asks.

"No David," Dawn replies. "I told you – don't worry."

"I just didn't know what to do."

"Do you now?"

"Do I now, what?"

"Do you know what to do?"

"I know what I want to do."

"And what do you want to do?"

David doesn't respond – he just sits there looking up at Dawn, and occasionally down at her open skirt.

"David?" Dawn interrupts.

"What?" Comes the quick response.

"If you can't tell me, maybe you should show me," Dawn pries, becoming more and more curious about what it is that David is thinking he wants to do, and wondering if it meets her own desires.

Yet David still doesn't reply, he simply pauses and breathes. And then, at last, he takes his hands off of his lap and places one on each of her knees. This first approach sends a quiver through her body and she stares intently at him, waiting for his next move. David focuses on the placement of his hands. With his fingers outstretched, he moves his hands forward – six inches to be exact – six inches up Dawn's legs and then back down to her knees, gently brushing her silken skin. Dawn shivers as David repeats the motion, over and over, and she watches David's hands carefully, before looking to his face.

David's eyes are fixed on the shadowy space between Dawn's legs. When he finally looks up at her, she is prepared, and gives an approving nod. With the next forward stroke, David's hands carefully disappear under Dawn's skirt. She spreads her legs wider as he slowly progresses up her inner thigh, searching for what lies in the darkness. Dawn jumps with a start, as David's hands stop advancing the moment that he reaches his mark. The two of them sit there staring at each other, and David begins tracing over Dawn's landing strip with his fingers. She feels the tickle of his gentle fingers inching along the strip of pubic hair, making their way to that point where the thin strip meets her pussy. Then without warning, Dawn grabs David's arms and pulls herself away from him. She slides off of the table and walks to the door.

"Um?" David utters. Confused, he stands up.

David's confusion is calmed when Dawn stops to lock the door, then turns back to him. She walks over to him and reaches up to put her arms around his neck, pausing for a moment to look into his blue eyes before pulling herself closer and kissing his motionless lips. David places his arms around Dawn and holds her tight as she gingerly pries his lips apart with her tongue. David's reaction is immediate and he opens his mouth wide – too wide at first, but eventually he is able to follow Dawn's lead and the kiss becomes deep and passionate. Much more passionate than Dawn had expected and she feels her head spin, and her body being swept away. David must be feeling something too because he lifts Dawn off of her feet, literally sweeping her away and carrying her to the far side of the room, pushing her back into the corner. Instantly, Dawn reaches down and grasps the growing bulge in David's tight jeans as he presses against her.

With the awkwardness of the start of that first kiss, Dawn suspects that David doesn't have a plan. Instead, David appears to be working off of instinct, which excites Dawn, and she braces herself for more surprises. Her hand is pinned between her body and David's pulsating bulge making it impossible for her to do much more than squeeze, but that seems to be enough. David begins a series of strained moans, punctuated with deep breaths as he pushes against Dawn's hand. Then suddenly, David drops to his knees in front of Dawn and lifts her skirt. Initially caught off guard, Dawn anticipates that the next thing that she will feel is David's tongue on her pussy, but that is not what she feels – not yet. Instead, David pulls Dawn's left leg over his one shoulder, and then her right leg over the other, lifting her off of the ground, and standing upright, holding her back against the corner and burying his face between her legs.

Dawn gasps as she feels David's lips touching her pussy. Then she wonders if this may be something new for David as she feels him lap haphazardly at her pussy with his tongue – like a dog drinking water – an unusually, devilishly thirsty dog. The excitement of the moment prevents Dawn from questioning David's approach, and at the same time she finds herself enjoying his unorthodox method. David is totally engulfed in what he is doing as he appears to be trying to lick every last inch of Dawn's pussy. His tongue moves in every direction – entering her pussy, brushing her clit, and even reaching her bum, tickling the tight hole. The sensation amazes Dawn and she interlocks her hands, holding the back of David's head.

David, seemingly still unable to focus on any one place to lick, moves his tongue vigorously. At times, he hits the perfect spot, and Dawn feels as if she will orgasm. And then, just as quickly, David's tongue moves, searching for the next pleasure point. The intensity of David's moans grows with each lap of his tongue, as his hands cup Dawn's butt cheeks, and one of his thumbs begins sliding in and out of her pussy. David positions his fingers to hold Dawn up, his tongue still thrashing about, and his thumb exploring her pussy. Dawn repositions herself slightly, concerned that, in her excitement, David may drop her from her precarious perch. In response, David adjusts his hand position again, eventually placing a finger against the puckered opening to Dawn's bum. Dawn isn't sure if what David does next is on purpose or accidental, but the sensation causes her to shudder as his middle finger enters her bum. There is no doubt that David also loves the sensation, and he begins to move his finger in time with his thumb, shyly at first, but then penetrating deeply into both of Dawn's holes. Dawn moves herself up and down, pressing against David's hand and mouth, her body aching for more.

Finally, David's tongue finds focus on Dawn's clit, and he begins licking and sucking the spot, causing her to shake uncontrollably. She looks down to watch David work as his moans transform into forceful grunts. His eyes are closed, and his brow is furled with a look of intensity. Dawn looks past David's face, as he thrusts his hips, pumping at the air, grunting with each forward motion. Dawn watches the bulge in David's jeans as it visibly throbs and she notices a small wet spot forming – then growing – and she realizes, he's cumming! David tenses, and his lower body quakes – his finger and thumb drive deep inside Dawn – his tongue presses hard on her clit. Dawn throws her arms over her head – pushing against the walls she arches her back, and her whole body begins to orgasm. Every muscle reacts to the power of the experience.

As their bodies relax, they hold their position, regaining composure, and then David slowly lowers Dawn to the ground. David is totally spent and breathing heavily, and as he stands Dawn reaches up and rubs her hand against the front of David's jeans, across the wet spot, and over the gradually shrinking bulge. David looks down at his wet jeans, and then at Dawn sitting in the corner, and he smiles at her, but says nothing. He reaches his hand out to her and helps her to stand, pulling her against himself as they stare at each other, close enough to kiss, but not.

"I should get going," David remarks, and he turns away, crossing the room and walking out door. Dawn watches him leave, and notices that he doesn't head to the shop, but instead, he walks out the front door – and keeps walking, not looking back.

"David?" Dawn says to herself as she moves across the room to the door. She stands there, unsure of what just happened, and wondering how she will explain David's leaving to Marshal Preston. A sudden chill reminds Dawn that she is standing, half naked, in front of the boardroom's open doorway, and she hurriedly pulls her skirt down into place. Grabbing David's forms off of the table, she rushes out of the room, not bothering to shut off the lights behind her. She drops the papers on her desk, before heading to the washroom to clean up and fix her hair and make-up.

1:34 PM

Having pulled herself together, Dawn returns to her desk and makes the call to Marshal Preston's office.

"Mr. Preston," Dawn calmly speaks into the phone. "I have David's forms here. But," she pauses for a second before finishing, "it seems that he has gone home sick or something. And I'm not sure if he will be back."

Dawn waits for Marshal Preston's rebuke. Instead, all she hears through the receiver is, "File the papers in case he comes back. Hopefully he won't. I never was too fond of the boy." And then the click of the phone as it's hung up.

Dawn stares at the telephone receiver for a moment before slamming it down.

"Well, I am fond of 'the boy'," she boasts.

Dawn copies David's phone number into her phone before filing the forms, planning to call him later to make sure everything is alright – and properly thank him for the rendezvous. Thinking about it reminds Dawn why she was in the boardroom in the first place – copier paper. As she turns to head back into the boardroom she hears the sound from her computer signalling an arriving email. She takes a quick glance at the screen and notices that it is an interoffice memo from Derek. Dawn rolls her eyes and mutters, "Now what?" as she opens the email.

Dawn

I want to apologize for my behavior during the few months that we've worked together. Especially some of the comments I've made to you. From the moment we met, I was overtaken by how beautiful and kind you are, but I immediately thought of how inferior I feel around you. I try to be funny and cool but always end up saying the stupid shit I say. I fall apart when I'm around you and my mouth just spews out the dumbest thing I can think of. I'm writing to you now, first because if I try to talk to you I'll screw it up, and second because while you were on vacation I missed seeing you around, and thought about how I could change the way I behave around you. As you can tell by our interaction earlier today, I failed in regard to any change. I just want to say that I am sorry. I'm trying, and I'll keep on trying until I get it right.

And as far as my boner showing... I can't help it. There is just something about being around you or thinking about you that causes my body to react like that. It just happens.

Thank you for listening. I will understand if

you just delete this message and still hate
me.

Derek

Re-reading those two words 'hate me',
Dawn thinks, I've never hated you. You just say the
creepiest things some times.

Dawn is touched by Derek's effort to make
amends, and as she leaves her desk to get the
copier paper, she is still thinking about what Derek
wrote. "Maybe I've been too hard on him."

4:15 PM

The afternoon has been rushing by, and Dawn's plan to leave early is in jeopardy. She ignores the clock and focuses on the task at hand, all the while knowing that a quiet dinner is likely not to happen. Once again, she refills the photocopier with paper, and repeats the process of adjusting a couple of settings, and hitting the 'Start' button. The copies start pouring from the machine. Dawn prepares the folders and binders that she requires, then starts putting each copy in its proper place, before filing the items away into drawers and onto shelves.

The task is taking much longer than she had hoped. People start flowing from the upstairs offices heading for the front door, indicating that it is now 4:30 and the work day is over. Just as quickly, the shop personnel file out of the building one by one. When the last copy runs through the machine, the copier beeps and then falls silent.

"Finally!" Dawn announces as she places the last pages into a binder, but the relief is short lived. There is no use rushing now, Dawn concedes, deciding that she will skip the quiet dinner and go straight from work to her photo shoot. Which now gives her time to get a head start on tomorrow, and she prepares to print off the long list of reports needed for the next day's meetings. With the printing started, all she has to do is wait. She chooses to use the time to check and see if anyone is still left upstairs. Dawn had once made the mistake of not checking before locking up for the night. She had been working after hours and assumed the building was empty. When she left, she armed the alarm system and locked the door. Marshal Preston was not impressed when the alarm started sounding. He was even less impressed at having to prove his identity to the police officers who responded to the alarm.

Dawn ascends the staircase to the second floor. Walking through the door at the top of the stairs she immediately notices the light on in Marshal Preston's office. To her right she can hear a couple of the engineers talking, and to her left she hears the clicking of keyboard keys coming from one of the cubicles by the window – Derek's cubicle. The email that Derek had sent earlier instantly comes to mind, but Dawn is still unsure of how to respond, although she is convinced that she wants to give Derek the benefit of the doubt. After some internal debate, Dawn decides that she will take this opportunity to respond to Derek in person. Marching toward the window, Dawn turns the corner into Derek's cubicle and stands, with arms crossed, beside his desk. Derek remains focused on his computer monitor, intently at work.

"I read your email," Dawn blurts out, announcing her presence and startling Derek. "I don't hate you."

Derek just looks up at Dawn, shaken by her unexpected visit. Recovering from the initial start, Derek lowers his head and says the only thing that comes to mind. "I've acted like an ass."

"If you're not really an ass, then stop being something you're not. Just be yourself."

"Shy, witless, and terrified around girls?" Derek sarcastically responds.

"It's better than being an ass. Your email was a complete shock. I never expected that from you. Why be so shy and terrified? You obviously have something inside of you that is just as attractive as the outside." Dawn pauses, realizing that she has just told Derek that he is attractive – something that she's seen but never thought she would express, because of Derek's childish behavior. However, the longer Dawn pauses, staring at a much more humble Derek, the more attractive he seems to become. Until finally she says, "You can't tell me that you don't see how attractive you are."

With that statement, Derek blushes. "Thank you Dawn."

Dawn looks down at the contrite man sitting in front of her and feels a certain remorse for forgetting that there was a time when she also felt shy, witless and terrified. She takes a seat on the edge of Derek's desk, not sure of what to say next. And as she sits there silently, looking at what appears to be a brand new Derek, she recognizes a little bit of the old Derek coming out. Or maybe it's just the most honest part of Derek. Whatever, there is no mistaking that distinctive shape on the front of Derek's pants. His boner is making another appearance.

"Derek?" Dawn asks. "Again?"

Derek looks down at the obvious and replies, "That is one thing I can't change. It's involuntary. It happened the first time I saw you, and it's happened every time since."

"Maybe if you wore tighter underwear it wouldn't be so noticeable," Dawn offers in the way of advice.

Derek laughs. "Maybe. I never thought about that."

"That's happened every time since the first time you saw me?" Dawn asks.

"Every time. And I'm not especially good at hiding it – as you know."

Try as she may, Dawn can't resist being amused by Derek's uncontrollable reaction to her presence. She is also unable to ignore the fact that she is feeling flattered – and, against all odds, somewhat stimulated herself. Just then Dawn hears the voices of the two engineers grow louder as they cross the room. She listens as the voices trail off down the stairs, and then disappear as the front door closes behind them on their way out, she ponders the present situation. It's just Derek and her left upstairs, with Marshal Preston tucked away in his oversized corner office. No longer unsure, Dawn turns to Derek, and without putting any further thought into it, she reaches down, and tugs on the button of Derek's pants. Caught off guard, Derek's only reaction is to grab hold of Dawn's hand and pull it away.

"I've only ever seen it through your pants," Dawn protests. "Can I see the real thing?"

Derek is initially stunned by the request, but responds truthfully, "I'd love for you to see. But what about Mr. Preston?"

"I don't think he wants to see," Dawn replies sarcastically.

"You know what I mean. He's still here. What if he catches me showing you my – my – you know."

"Marshal, is sitting in there," Dawn responds motioning toward Marshal Preston's office. "He'll be focused on what he's doing. Could be work, video games, porn – who knows, but he won't leave his office for quite a while. You've been here long enough to know that he's almost always the last to leave." And Dawn thinks for a moment about why that is. "If you knew his life, you'd understand why he prefers to hang out late after work."

Derek thinks for a moment, then says timidly, "Okay, but I'm telling you up front, it's not very impressive." He closes his eyes and grabs a hold of the arms of his chair as if bracing for a major collision."You can look."

Dawn avoids laughing out loud and is reminded of how cute Derek can actually be when he's not being an ass. She takes a quick look over her shoulder to make sure that Marshal Preston hasn't wandered out of his office. Re-assured that there won't be any interruptions, she reaches once again for Derek's button, this time she unfastens it carefully. Pausing for effect, she continues by clasping Derek's zipper with two fingers and slowly pulling it down, opening the front of his pants. Dawn surprises herself as she feels excitement brought on by this paced reveal. Using both hands, she grabs the top of Derek's boxers, holding for a moment, before gingerly pulling the boxers up and over his boner. The erection bounds from Derek's pants as if it had been anxiously waiting for someone to finally set it free.

Dawn sits up straight on the edge of the desk, crosses her arms and thoughtfully studies what has been revealed. The first thing that she notices is Derek's earthy, natural appearance, represented by the bushy tuft encircling the base of his erection. The temptation is too great for Dawn, and she reaches down, running a finger through the frizzy thatch. She is surprised by it's softness and thinks that, although Derek may not trim, it is quite possible that he shampoos and conditions. She pulls away as Derek opens one eye and looks down at his exposed boner, then up at her, expecting some sort of negative reaction, or belittling expression. But Dawn is smiling, and not in a cruel way – a genuine, positive smile. He opens both eyes and looks back and forth between his boner and Dawn's smile, waiting for her to say something.

"What?" Derek finally asks, becoming increasingly uncertain as to what Dawn is truly thinking.

"Maybe the size isn't impressive by some standards," Dawn answers honestly, noticing it's length of about four and a half inches. "But the shape and the curve – and the cute mushroom head – it's very nice Derek."

Derek looks relieved, but is still experiencing some doubt.

"Really?" he inquires. "But it's so..."

"It's very nice," Dawn interrupts.

"Thank you." Derek shyly accepts the compliment, suddenly feeling a sense of pride.

Satisfied that Dawn has seen and approved, he reaches down to hide his boner safely away in his pants, but Dawn grabs his arm.

"Wait," she says, taking another quick look over her shoulder. "Maybe if I helped you with this boner, you wouldn't keep getting them every time you see me."

"Help?" Derek asks, puzzled.

"You know – *help*," Dawn explains, emphasizing '*help*'.

"You mean..."

"I mean, jerk you off."

"Here?"

"Yes, here."

"Now?"

"Yes, now."

Derek considers the proposition realizing that he is somewhat embarrassed to admit the truth that finally comes out. "You are the first girl that has even seen it." Dawn doesn't flinch making it impossible for Derek to detect any sort of understanding from her. "I've never been touched." Still, no response from Dawn. "The only person I've ever been with is myself."

Dawn does understand, but has held back, allowing Derek to finally be himself. Then she leans in and softly whispers, "I would like to touch you, Derek. Would you like me to touch you?"

Derek submits. "Yes."

Dawn agrees with a smile, "Alright." And she leans over, reaching out her hand.

Derek once again grabs a hold of the arms of his chair. And Dawn, once again, avoids laughing out loud. Derek's eyes are wide open and flash back and forth between his boner and Dawn, as she grabs hold, the width of her hand almost engulfing his full length. She begins stroking – the short strokes reaching from the base and up across the head. Derek watches her hand intently, not quite believing what is happening. Dawn leans in further and reaches out with her other hand, cupping Derek's balls. This causes Derek to tilt his head back, and he looks up at the ceiling momentarily before looking back down and watching both of Dawn's hands at work on him – one stroking his boner – the other massaging his balls. He starts to fidget in his chair, still holding tightly to the arms.

"Um... um... I don't know about this," he says.

Dawn lets go of him. "Do you want me to stop?" she asks.

"No... no I don't," he replies, his voice quivering. "But," he pauses, shyly looking at Dawn with a nervous smile on his face. "I'm going to cum."

"I can stop if you don't want to cum."

"No, don't stop Dawn. Please don't stop."

Dawn grins and takes hold of Derek's boner and balls again. She resumes stroking and massaging.

"Oh Dawn," Derek whimpers, slightly lifting himself off of the chair. "Oh – oh Dawn."

"You might want to open your shirt." Dawn advises Derek.

"Okay." Derek quickly pulls at his shirt buttons, from the bottom up. He's biting his bottom lip now and moaning. Dawn continues her slow steady pace watching Derek frantically attempting to get his shirt open. He can't get to the top button that is hidden under his tie, which now lies across his bare chest and stomach, but he is out of time. He grabs the arms of the chair once more and leans back as far as he can, arching his back. He looks straight into Dawn's eyes and says one word, "Dawn." Then closing his eyes he throws his head back, with a grunt.

Dawn looks down as Derek throbs in her hand and she is surprised by the first shot of cum. It shoots across Derek's stomach and chest, leaving a white line along the center of his black tie, from the knot down to the tip. The next stroke releases another powerful stream of cum. And then a third. Derek's tie now looks like a work of abstract art, and cum runs over his stomach, chest and Dawn's hands. Dawn continues her firm grasp and slow, steady motion, each stroke releasing more and more, but even as the quantity begins to dwindle, she is beginning to think that Derek will never stop cumming, and she wonders how long he has been saving up for something like this. At last the flow subsides, and Dawn gently cradles Derek's balls and softening penis in her hands, allowing him to fully enjoy the moment as much as she has.

"Finally, Derek doesn't have a boner."

Derek looks down at his soft penis nestled in Dawn's hand, and he shudders, laughing quietly. Dawn laughs along with him, grabbing some tissues from the box on the desk. She wipes the cum off of her hands, and then helps Derek cleanup as he pulls at his tie to remove it.

"That was amazing!" Derek exclaims.

"It was pretty impressive," Dawn admits, still wiping off more cum and tossing tissue after tissue into the garbage can under Derek's desk.

Finally cleaned off, Derek tosses his tie into the garbage can, as well. "Maybe I should stop wearing ties every day."

"I don't know," Dawn says. "I think they suit you."

"Dawn," Derek sheepishly continues, "thanks for giving me a second chance."

"You should give yourself a second chance," Dawn replies. "I like the real you a lot better."

"Me too." And he tucks his penis back into his boxers and fastens his pants.

"Maybe now you won't get a boner every time you see me."

Derek looks down at his pants blushing. "Yeah."

"But if it does pop up," Dawn teases. "Maybe I'll have to *help* you with it again."

Derek's relaxed expression changes quickly and he looks up at Dawn. "Really?"

Almost instantly, Dawn notices a rise in the front of Derek's pants.

"Derek!"

Derek looks down at his growing boner and shakes his head. "Sorry. Maybe I just need to start wearing tighter underwear."

Dawn simply laughs, shakes her head and walks away. Her mood quickly changes from playful to frantic as she looks up at the clock on the wall and realizes that she is going to be late for her photo shoot. She hurries down the stairs to her desk.

First shoot in weeks and I'm going to blow it by being late, Dawn thinks. She hurriedly grabs the papers from her printer and tosses them aside on her desk. Opening the closest door, she pulls out her bag of fresh clothes. With no time to seek out privacy, she strips off her skirt and top right there in the office, and hastily replaces them with a short jean skirt and tank top. She rushes around turning off lights and shutting down her computer, then runs out the front door into the parking lot. Suddenly realizing that she hasn't called a cab, she reaches into her purse and digs around for her phone, muttering to herself. "I'm definitely going to be late if I have to wait for a cab."

As she searches for the phone, Derek walks out of the building and Dawn turns her attention to him.

"Are you leaving?" she asks.

Derek replies with an observation, "You've changed."

"I need a ride to my photo shoot," Dawn informs him.

"Photo shoot?"

"Yes, photo shoot!"

Derek, still puzzled, blankly stares at Dawn.

"I model! I have a photo shoot!" Dawn tries to explain.

"Oh, okay," Derek relents. "I didn't know you are a model."

Still not getting across the importance of what she is saying, Dawn presses, "I don't have time to explain now. Can you give me a drive or not?"

"Sure, no problem," Derek agrees.

"Thank you!" Dawn exclaims, and she kisses Derek on the cheek. "I need to be there in less than fifteen minutes."

"Well, where are we going?" Derek asks.

"Downtown."

"I don't know if I can make that in fifteen minutes."

"Promise you'll get me there in less than fifteen minutes, and I'll *help* you with that on the way." Dawn motions toward Derek's everlasting boner.

"I promise – less than fifteen minutes – I promise!" Derek declares as he sprints across the parking lot.

As they rush to Derek's car, Dawn reaches into her purse and pulls out some tissues, handing them to Derek. "You'll need these." And she reminds him, "Less than fifteen minutes, Derek."

"I promise!" Derek replies as he and Dawn climb into the car. Within seconds, they are on their way – Dawn to her photo shoot and Derek to another climax.

Thirteen minutes later they pull up to the curb in front of the building where Dawn's photo shoot is taking place. Dawn jumps out of the car and rushes to the nearest entrance, leaving Derek sitting in the car, wiping the steering wheel and his shirt with the tissues.

He calls out to Dawn, "Do you need a ride home later?"

Dawn turns to look back as she opens the door. "I'm not sure when I'll be finished. I'll call a cab. See you at work tomorrow. Thanks for the ride." And with that she disappears into the building.

"Thank you." Derek smiles, still wiping his shirt.

5:41 PM

Resting in the downtown core, the building is an old converted factory – now the home of a variety of studios. Artist studios, film studios, recording studios and photo studios. One of the large photo studios in the rear of the building is where Dawn is headed. She normally wouldn't worry about being a little bit late for a photo shoot. Every time she's arrived early or even right on time, she has been left waiting as the photographer makes endless adjustments to his equipment or sets. However, this photographer is a friend that she has done a number of shoots with in the past. She is also aware that this shoot requires almost two hours of preparation. Her and the other models are to be painted head to toe with body paint, and two artists have been hired to paint the group – two artists that are on the clock.

Dawn takes the stairs to the third floor, walks down the long corridor and opens the door to the studio. Her friend greets her enthusiastically with a hug.

"Dawn!" Paul exclaims.

Paul is a sweetheart. The first time Paul and Dawn shot together was twelve years ago. He was one of Dawn's first photographers, and he taught her a lot about the business. Paul had already been shooting for twenty years, and knew the ins and outs of the art world. He's a big, kind, teddy bear of a man, sporting a neatly trimmed beard. Dawn's never seen Paul outside of the studio, and she knows very little about the rest of his life, other than the fact that he's an admired photographer in the local art community, and at one time, Paul had been married, years before Dawn ever met him. The conversations that they have shared have always revolved around photography, art, and whatever shoot they were working on at the time.

"Hi Paul, I'm a little late," Dawn apologizes. "Sorry."

"Don't worry," Paul assures her. "I've just been setting up while the painters paint the men." He points to a doorway leading to a smaller room off to the side of the studio. "This will be perfect. I know it. Everything is in place."

Paul's enthusiasm is comforting. His vision for this shoot requires a central girl – Dawn – and three male models. The backdrop is a large mural of a forest during autumn, donated by a local artist for this shoot. The men will be painted to look like trees, matching those in the forest mural. Dawn is to be painted to resemble the red and gold leaves. The only part of any of them that won't be painted is their faces and their hands. Paul says that the visible expression of the faces and hands will show the trees and leaves as living objects. Not becoming overly metaphysical in her interpretation of art, Dawn imagines that the result will look stunning.

The body painting is something new to Dawn, so this isn't a typical shoot for her, but things are never typical when she shoots with Paul. Paul will spend months on a concept, choosing just the right scenery, costumes, make-up – and models. Dawn is a favorite of Paul's, when it comes to models, and he works her in to whatever shoot he can. In turn, Dawn has been offering her modeling services at no charge for Paul's shoots, including this one.

However, the other three models she'll be working with, are being paid and will have gone through a meticulous screening process. To fulfill the vision, Paul has laid out strict criteria for the models. The men must be tall and slender, but muscular, without being bulky. They must have short dark hair or a shaved head, and no facial hair. No tattoos or body modifications that may show through the body paint are allowed on any of the models. And all of them must have a smooth canvas for the body artists to paint on – meaning no body hair – anywhere. Dawn hasn't met the men yet, but Paul has informed her that he has found three male models that fit the bill perfectly.

"Dawn," Paul continues, "let me take you in the back and introduce you to the models who will be working with you. The artists will be ready to paint you soon."

"Okay, I'm ready," Dawn replies, following Paul's lead.

Entering the small room, Paul exclaims majestically, "Everyone! This is Dawn!" He then continues the introductions, as Dawn enters behind him. "Dawn! These are our artists, Brad and Leah!" Paul points to the slender young couple crouched on the floor. Dawn is instantly struck by how the two seem to have such an 'artistic' look about them. Their clothes are the first thing that she notices – faded blue jeans and loose fitting, plain white t-shirts, spotted with dashes of color from their work. Both have long, straight, dark hair that hangs loosely, partially covering the sides of their thin faces. Brad's face is further obscured by a full mustache and goatee. Leah doesn't appear to be wearing any make-up at all, revealing a natural beauty of fine skin and delicate features.

"They are the best husband/wife team in the medium." Sticking with his grandiose style, Paul turns to the other men in the room. "And these are the other models – Jason, Randy and Patrick!"

Looking slightly humbled by Paul's ambitious introduction, the three men stand in the middle of the room – naked, but with various stages of body paint already applied. Their features are what Dawn would expect. Attractive, toned, well defined, but their ages are a guess. In the modeling world, everyone is ageless. Many try to hide their real age for fear that they won't receive as much work. Dawn has no idea how old these other three models claim to be, but she makes a decision as she looks them over. Jason is around her age – a little younger – probably twenty-eight. Randy, however, is older – maybe thirty-nine. And Patrick is younger than all of them – Dawn guesses twenty-two.

"How much longer?" Paul asks Brad and Leah.

"Give us another twenty minutes with the guys," replies Brad. "And we'll need about an hour and a half with Dawn."

"Alright then!" Paul claps his hands loudly. "I will see you all when your transformation is complete." And he struts out of the room.

5:58 PM

"You can sit over there," Brad says to Dawn, motioning to a small chair sitting off to one side of the room. "We won't be too much longer." And he and Leah go back to work.

"Thanks," Dawn replies, taking a seat and placing her bags on the floor under the chair. "I've never seen how this is done."

"You've never been painted before?" Leah asks.

"No."

"Well, first we cover the body with a base coat," Brad explains, "using the different colors and shades that we're looking for. We use a wide spray on the airbrush gun. Then we fill in the details with a finer stream on most of the body. For the sensitive areas," he points to Jason's penis, "we use a paint brush. The fine spray from the gun would be too harsh."

As Dawn listens to the explanation, she takes in all that she is seeing. A number of photos, taken of the mural, lie scattered around. They're obviously trying to imitate the forest closely. The base coat on the men must be complete because Brad and Leah are both working on details – Brad with the airbrush gun and Leah with a paint brush. Dawn observes the process closely, intrigued by the artistry and skill of the painters, but also somewhat titillated by the idea of a human canvas.

The three models seem to fit Paul's criteria to a tee. All are over six feet tall, their bodies undeniably muscular, but lean, and they have dark, short hair – except Jason, who's head is shaved. Dawn also notices that not a hair can be seen on their bodies – anywhere. Their smooth bodies are covered with shades of green and brown, and Dawn visualizes for a moment what each of them would look like without a coat of paint. Some things can't be hidden by a coat of paint, such as shape and size – particularly pertaining to certain body parts. Dawn finds herself admiring three exceptionally lovely penis'. In their soft state, she knows that she's only seeing half of the picture. Once hard everything changes – size and shape. Some men change very little in size when they become erect, while others show significant growth. And as she scans Jason's penis, all she can think is, if Jason is that large right now – and she swallows hard. Suddenly Dawn is aware that Jason and Randy are watching her watch them, and she looks away, blushing at being caught staring. She distracts herself by looking toward Leah.

"Hold still!" Leah is experiencing a little difficulty as Patrick's penis seems to jump occasionally at the touch of her paintbrush.

"I can't help it!" Patrick sighs.

"You won't like it if I have to use the gun."

Dawn, Randy, Jason and Brad, all laugh as Patrick stands straight, looking up at the ceiling, trying to focus on something else other than the soft paintbrush. It works, and Brad and Leah are able to finish the detailing without further interruption. The men step aside, admiring the artwork on their bodies.

"Don't sit down or brush against anything," Brad instructs the men. "Just stand there and give the paint some time to set properly."

They do as they are told and stand off to the side.

"Your turn Dawn," Brad calls to her. "Just stand here and we'll get you done."

Dawn stands and begins to undress. As she does she comes to an uncomfortable realization. It's not being nude in front of all of these people, Dawn is quite comfortable nude. And getting undressed in front of others doesn't phase her in the least, but as she pulls off her skirt and stands naked in front of Brad and Leah, she looks down – and there it is – her stripe. She remembers what Paul had said about a 'smooth canvas'. Of course, Brad and Leah notice right away. Then the other models notice. All eyes are suddenly on Dawn's stripe. Dawn looks at Leah. "I forgot – and I didn't bring a razor."

"I have a razor," Leah replies. "But I only use it to remove a little arm or leg hair on models. I don't have any shaving creme. Do you want to go to the shower and use some soap or something?"

Dawn thinks for a moment. The shower is down one flight of stairs and at the other end of the building. Looking at a clock on the wall she realizes how late the shoot will be set back because of the delay. It's far too much trouble. "Just shave it," she says.

"Are you sure?"

"Yeah. Just be careful."

"Alright. Don't worry, I'll be very careful." Leah pulls a razor out of one of her bags. She inserts a new blade and moves toward Dawn.

Dawn isn't worried about her stripe, although it has been there for most of her adult life. Nor is she concerned about a little dry shave. However, being shaved, by a woman, and in front of four guys, is something she can't say she's ever experienced before. She feels a little uneasy with everyone watching as Leah approaches the stripe with the razor. Dawn tries to make eye contact with the men, hoping that it will take some of the focus off of what Leah is doing, but Jason, Randy, Patrick, and even Brad, are intent on watching the removal of Dawn's landing strip.

"Everybody have a good view?" Dawn jokes, causing all of the men to look away momentarily– all except Patrick, who actually repositions himself for a better view. A few seconds later, the other men's eyes have drifted back to Dawn. Leah moves cautiously with the first swipe of the razor and looks up at Dawn to make sure that everything is still okay. Their eyes meet and Dawn motions with a nod at the men in the room. Leah snickers as she looks over to see all eyes on Dawn's disappearing strip of hair. Looking back up, Leah watches as Dawn lifts her arms and stretches out her body, allowing an unobstructed view of the proceedings.

Leah, just as intrigued by the sudden attention, especially from her husband, takes another swipe at Dawn's stripe. Slowly and methodically, Leah removes every last remnant of Dawn's landing strip and places the razor on the floor. Dawn looks down and has the sensation of being more naked than she has ever been before. She relaxes her body and lowers her hands touching the spot where the hair had been, feeling the smooth skin. Partly out of curiosity as to how it feels, but also to tease the gawking men, Dawn runs her finger down the newly shaved spot until she reaches the tip of her pussy, and then back up to the place where her landing strip had stretched. Repeating the motion a few times, examining and teasing with her finger, Dawn notices she has even attracted Leah's gaze.

"Perfect." Dawn smiles. "Ready for paint!"

The sudden statement startles the other models, and they look away quickly in an unsuccessful attempt to hide they're leering. They are also unsuccessful at hiding the slight swelling that has occurred below their waists while they were watching. Dawn's smile grows and she covers her mouth with her hand, restraining a giggle. Randy, Jason, and Patrick, who have drifted closer, step back and turn away, as Brad fumbles on the ground for his air gun. Leah joins Dawn in her amusement while placing the razor back in her bag and pulling out some fresh brushes. With composure returning to the room, Brad begins spraying a base coat on to Dawn's body as Leah prepares the brushes and other guns for the detailing.

Dawn stands perfectly still, only twisting and turning her body slightly on Brad's direction as he coats every inch of her with layers of paint. Brad is working quickly, using the spray gun in long, sweeping strokes, starting at Dawn's feet and moving up her body. Before too long, he has made it as far up as Dawn's breasts. The sudden blast of air mixed with the cool paint causes her nipples to react extraordinarily, and they quickly harden, coming to full attention. This seems to delight the male models who are looking on intently and smiling devilishly. Brad, behaving professionally, ignores the reaction and continues to paint, finishing with Dawn's shoulders and neck.

"That's all for the base coat," Brad explains as he puts down the air gun. "Would you like to walk around and stretch for a bit before we start the detailing?"

"I'm okay. You can keep going," Dawn tells them. "But, could I make a brief phone call while you continue?"

"Sure," Leah replies. "We'll start with your legs and work our way up again."

"Thanks." Dawn walks over and retrieves her phone from her purse, then stands back in place in the middle of the room. Brad and Leah each have their air guns and start spraying fine lines onto Dawn's legs. The stream of air is much more acutely directed, and Dawn finds the pressure a little irritating, but she doesn't flinch, instead her focus is on browsing through her phone to find the number that she's looking for. The number found and dialed, Dawn places the phone to her ear, waiting for an answer. Everyone in the room is silent and listens to Dawn's half of the conversation.

"David? – It's Dawn from KPR. – Oh, I'm just standing around. – Good, thank you. How are you doing? – That's good I was a little worried. – Well you left so suddenly. – You were? – Oh I see. I understand. – I hope everything goes well for you then. – Sure. What? – Yeah! I'd love that. We can takeover from where we left off. – Sounds good. You have my number now. Give me a call. – Alright. Take care. I'll talk to you soon."

Dawn ends the call satisfied that everything is well with David, and happy that it wasn't something she had said or done to make him run off. David was planning on leaving anyway. It's easy to understand how working in the shop at KPR isn't ideal for a young man with his whole life ahead. It's also a welcome surprise to hear that he would like to get together outside of work. That's something to look forward to – sounds promising. Dawn can't help but grin as she hands her phone to Jason. "Could you put this over by my bags please?"

Jason takes the phone and places it on Dawn's purse as the body painting continues. The detailing takes longer, and the time is used by everyone to get to know each other. A discussion about the photo shoot begins, and the four models put on their best 'professional' faces. The rest of the painting procedure moves along without interruption. Except for the brief moment when Leah uses the brush to complete the detailing around, and on, Dawn's newly trimmed 'sensitive area'. Leah moves the brush slowly and purposely over the outer edges of Dawn's pussy, enjoying the way the tickle of the brush causes Dawn to shiver, and causes the men to awkwardly stare. Again, all eyes are on Dawn, apparently enjoying this part of the painting, as much as they enjoyed the shaving.

"Almost done?" Brad interrupts.

"Yes!" Leah snaps back with a glare. And a few seconds later she reveals, "Done!"

Dawn walks over to the full length mirror on the wall and examines her new appearance. Her body looks like a bed of fallen leaves. The effect is so life like that she pinches at a couple of places on her skin as if she could lift an individual leaf off of herself.

"This is gorgeous!"

Dawn's compliment seems to relax Leah's apparent feeling of pressure – of schedules – of time lines and she coyly responds, "I'm so glad that you like it."

Brad checks the time, ignoring the polite exchange of pleasantries between the ladies and reminds himself that they're falling behind schedule.

Looking to the male models, Brad focuses on his not being a disappointment to Paul, and he directs the men. "Alright guys, you're finished. I don't want to keep Paul waiting any longer." Then turning to Leah he suggests, "You should touch-up Dawn's make-up while the rest of the paint sets. I'll take the guys out and show Paul what we've accomplished."

"Tell him, we won't be long." Leah nods politely to her husband as he exits behind the others, pulling the door closed on his way.

Dawn continues to stand in front of the mirror admiring the finished artwork, seemingly oblivious to the conversation that has taken place behind her, and the exit of everyone but Leah. Looking past her own reflection, she catches a glimpse of Leah sitting on the floor a few feet behind her. Leah also seems to be admiring the artwork, but the look in her eyes gives Dawn the impression that it's more than the artwork that she is admiring.

"I guess you should work on my make-up," Dawn says, turning toward Leah. "Paul will be wanting me out there soon."

Leah turns away, nervously fumbling for her make-up case. "Yes, um, I just need a few things from my kit."

While Leah opens the case and begins retrieving brushes and powders from inside, Dawn silently steps closer to her. Leah places a brush or two beside a few canisters of powder that she has laid on a nearby stool. Then taking a brush and powder container in hand, she stands and finds herself face to face with Dawn. There is a brief pause before Leah dips the brush into the powder and says, "Let me just even out your make-up a little. Close your eyes. This powder is pretty loose and may fly around a bit."

"Alright," Dawn responds, closing her eyes as Leah begins to gently dab her face with the brush. "I hope you weren't too embarrassed having to shave me earlier." Dawn's innocent comment sparks an immediate reaction from Leah, and Dawn feels the brush come to an abrupt stop on her cheek, but eventually pick up again as she hears Leah's voice.

"No – not at all."

The reaction and stuttered response from Leah is intriguing to Dawn and she pursues further reaction. "The guys sure seemed to make a big deal about it."

"Well you know how they can be. It's kind of silly – isn't it?"

"Yeah it is – it looked like they were getting a little aroused."

"They weren't the only ones." And even as the words leave her mouth, Leah realizes what she has just said. The brush stops again, drawing a grin from Dawn, who is well aware of the implications of Leah's statement.

"You too?" Dawn asks.

"Me too – what?"

"You found it arousing?"

"The part after I was done shaving you." Leah continues hesitantly, finding it difficult to concentrate on evenly applying the powder to Dawn's face. "You looked so soft – you touched yourself – I wanted to as well."

Dawn opens her eyes and looks directly at Leah. "Have you ever..." And as she closes her eyes again she finishes the question, "touched a woman?"

Leah doesn't hesitate with the answer to this question, quickly expressing a quiet, "No."

"It's too bad that I'm covered in paint right now," Dawn teases. "A touch might mess up the design."

"Yes – it would."

"But, you're not covered in paint."

"No – I'm not."

Dawn agrees, "No – you're not."

With her eyes still closed Dawn reaches out and places her hands on Leah's hips, holding her for a moment before feeling her way to the button on Leah's jeans. Once there, she carefully opens the button and slides the zipper all of the way down. Her fingers feel the material of Leah's simple, cotton panties that are obviously worn for comfort and not show. Yet at this point, with her hands being her eyes, Dawn finds the panties extremely sexy, and she moves toward discovering what lies hidden beneath the cotton. Placing the palm of her hand on Leah's stomach, she slides her fingers down, making her way past the elastic. Seconds later, Dawn makes her first discovery – Leah is completely shaved. At the same time, she realizes that she hasn't felt the touch of Leah's make-up brush on her face in some time and she opens her eyes.

Leah is still holding the brush and powder in her hands, but they hang in the air, inactive. Her eyes are closed and her mouth is open slightly, lips quivering as she breathes deeply. Dawn watches Leah's face closely and continues deeper into the cotton panties. Leah's jeans are tight, making it difficult for Dawn to move her hand and fingers, but encouraged by Leah's begging expression she finds her way to warmth and moisture. The expectant touch of Dawn's finger draws a shudder from Leah – and finger meeting clit elicits a response equaling a dream fulfilled. So satisfying is the response, that Dawn considers just leaving it at that and not pressing further, but as she stares at Leah's face, while her finger gently moves across Leah's clit, Dawn determines that it is up to Leah to decide – and there is no indication from Leah that this should end now.

Using her free hand, Dawn inches her way under Leah's t-shirt and up her side, feeling tiny goose-bumps form on Leah's skin along the progression, until her fingertips feel the gentle curve of a breast. As she brushes each of her fingers over Leah's excited nipple, she watches her invitingly run her tongue over her lips. Dawn leans forward, taking full advantage of the invitation – and Leah's mouth. Leah melts under Dawn's kiss and drops the brush and powder. Dawn listens as each hit the floor, immediately followed by the sound of the opening door. Quickly, Dawn spins, turning Leah's back to the door just as Brad walks into the room.

"Leah! Are you done with Dawn's make-up yet?" He forcefully asks as he enters.

Leah's response is immediate, more forceful, but simple. "In a minute, Brad!"

Brad steps back, caught off guard by what he perceives to be an unjust outburst from his wife, but before he can say anything more he is made aware that his wife is not quite finished asserting her disapproval of the interruption.

"I'll tell you when I'm done!"

Dawn covertly slips her hand out of Leah's shirt and inconspicuously buttons Leah's jeans while distracting Brad, looking directly at him and calmly saying, "Yup, we're done Brad." Then looking Leah in the eyes, she adds with a whisper, "For now."

Dawn steps around Leah and slips by Brad who is still standing in the open doorway. Leah spins around and marches toward the door, pushing past Brad and sneering at him, as she follows Dawn. Brad seems stunned, but with an uncaring shrug of his shoulders, he pulls the door closed behind him as he follows the ladies.

8:02 PM

Paul has been spending the time scattering leaves on the floor in front of the mural, extending the forest out into the open room. Dawn notices Jason, Randy and Patrick standing to the side, against the wall, passively watching as Paul works to prepare the scene. Aware of the intricate designs displayed on her body, and in awe of the extravagance of the setting laid out before her, Dawn feels that if she were to lie amongst the leaves, she would blend in so perfectly that she may just fade away.

As if spurned on by the appearance of his leading lady, Paul stops what he is doing. Pausing to examine all of the models he exclaims, "Wonderful! Brad and Leah, you have captured the essence of the forest so well! Everyone move over here!" Paul enthusiastically instructs, pointing to the area by the mural.

The models politely thank Brad and Leah, then carefully walk onto the carpet of leaves as the two artists return to the small room to clean their tools and pack up the equipment. Paul has the three men line up beside each other, in front of the mural. Randy and Patrick are moved to either side of Jason. With a snicker, Dawn wonders if it is Jason's bald head or large penis that earns him the center spot. Paul then asks the men to kneel on one leg and directs Dawn to lie down in their outstretched arms.

"Now lift her ever so gently over your heads," Paul directs.

The men struggle to coordinate the lift, but find that lifting Dawn simultaneously is awkward. They decide that the easiest way to accomplish the move is for Jason to pick Dawn up and lift her as high as he can so that Randy and Patrick can position themselves and help with the rest of the lift. Jason literally sweeps Dawn off of her feet, as if he were about to carry a bride over the threshold. Once in Jason's arms, Dawn stretches out as straight as she can, allowing Patrick to grab her legs and Randy, her neck and shoulders. As the three men lift Dawn as high as they can over their heads, she experiences a sudden rush, feeling secure in the care of the three men.

Dawn has always enjoyed the sexual aspect of modeling. Especially nude modeling. Being completely nude and open while someone studies your body carefully through the lens of a camera, causes feelings of exhilaration and often titillation. Dawn has posed with other female models, and the occasional male, but this is the first time that she has been in a photo shoot with more than one other person. And as the three strong, attractive, male models place their hands on her body and lift her, Dawn feels the excitement rise with her body. She stretches out on her back, completely trusting the hands that grasp her, with only a thin layer of paint between them and her flesh.

Patrick has one hand on Dawn's right calf and the other on her left hamstring. Randy holds the back of Dawn's neck, and her spine between her shoulder blades. Jason's right hand is placed in the small of Dawn's back, his left hand cups Dawn's left butt cheek, with his fingers resting precariously close to her pussy. It is Jason's left hand and fingers that are most guilty of making concentration difficult for Dawn, but she forces herself to focus on the scene that Paul is attempting to capture within his camera. And what Paul sees through his lens is three trees standing with their strong limbs reaching for the sky under a canopy of red and gold leaves.

"Perfect!" Paul declares. "My God, it's beautiful! Hold her! Just try to hold her. Dawn, I need movement – expression with your body. Find your poses. I want to experience movement in the leaves."

Paul pushes a button on the stereo in the corner and the room fills with the music that he has chosen to set the mood and inspire his vision. Dawn recognizes the song as an Eva Cassidy version of 'Autumn Leaves' and she is immediately stirred. She begins purposely moving to the sorrowful tune, careful not to move too fast or too far, thinking of the three men who must remain trees with sturdy limbs. They are doing an exceptional job maintaining their stance and stature, allowing Dawn to move freely from pose to pose, the strong hands beneath her, carrying her weight and adjusting to each movement. The flashes of the lights come fast as Paul captures image after image, pouring praise on all of his models with each shot.

After fifteen minutes and a few dozen photos, Paul stops the music and calls for a break, allowing the men to put Dawn down, and rest. He wanders over to a table containing some cables and a small monitor. Plugging a cable into the camera he prepares to preview the images he's taken, while the models chat.

"How are you doing?" Dawn asks the three guys after her feet are back on the ground.

They are all massaging their arms and flexing their fingers.

"It's alright, Dawn," Jason replies. "You're doing a great job. We'll survive."

"Well, don't let Paul push you too hard," Dawn reminds them. "He can get a little obsessive. Especially when things are working out the way he's envisioned them."

"We only have a few more sets to get through," Randy assures her. "It's not like it's all bad. We get to hold you."

Dawn responds with a smile to the compliment. "Well I'm glad that you're able to have some fun with it."

"Everyone rested?" Paul interjects, having reviewed what he's shot and ready to continue, not actually looking for a response from his models. "I think I've captured the shots I want. I still want to do at least one more set – a 'just in case' set. Let's position in a similar manner and see if we stumble across something new and unexpected."

Paul's announcement of only having to do one more set breathes new life into the models. Jason, Randy and Patrick step forward, moving into place, and preparing to repeat the same routine of lifting Dawn, as she moves onto the bed of leaves and toward Jason. However, this time Dawn doesn't wait to be swept off of her feet, instead choosing to leap up, making Jason catch her as she lifts her arms in the air in a playful, diva pose. Immediately, the atmosphere of the room relaxes, and the four models are able to laugh together. Dawn is lifted as before, and Paul restarts the music. Feeling more confident and even more assured of the hands holding her up, Dawn moves much more freely. The men hold Dawn, constantly adjusting to her exuberant motion, and occasionally looking up to admire her writhing body.

Jason's left hand is once again in position on Dawn's butt cheek, and at one point, as Dawn moves her hips, Jason's precariously positioned fingers brush the edge of Dawn's pussy. The sudden sensation causes Dawn to pause, but her pause is interrupted as Jason's fingers brush across her pussy a second time. This time it appears to be much more purposeful. Dawn moves again, no longer focused on a pose, but focused on repeating the recently discovered sensation and determining whether or not Jason's act was accidental or deliberate. At the same time, Jason is wondering if Dawn's movements are an invitation to be touched, and he adjusts his hand, positioning his fingers directly between her legs, yet not touching. However, Dawn's movement pushes her pussy toward Jason's fingers and they meet firmly.

That was deliberate, they both think, but neither of them protest. Instead , Dawn cautiously allows her new friend to pursue more, wondering how far Jason will go. The answer comes quickly as Jason begins massaging Dawn's clit with his forefinger. Desiring to indicate acceptance, and equally wanting to encourage more, Dawn moves in motion to Jason's finger. The response is immediate, as Jason takes things further, inserting his middle finger into Dawn's pussy, and causing Dawn's movements to become more extraneous, catching the attention of Randy. First Randy looks at Dawn to get some indication as to why her movements have changed so drastically, but from where he is situated, all he can see is the moving leaves painted on Dawn's body. Randy looks to Patrick who is staring straight forward, obviously trying to stay focused under the added pressure of what he assumes are simply enthusiastic poses. Eventually, Patrick looks at Randy, and observes him mouthing the words. "What the hell?"

Patrick looks up at Dawn, starting to wonder the same thing as Randy. Having a much better vantage point, Patrick can see exactly what is causing Dawn's extra movement. Jason, ever the professional, gives no sign of his part in things, staring straight ahead, intermittently closing his eyes in an attempt to stay focused on what he's doing to Dawn, as well as what he is supposed to be doing for the camera. Patrick, however, becomes transfixed on the spot between Dawn's legs, watching intently as Jason massages Dawn's clit and penetrates her pussy with his finger. It's all Patrick can see – it's all he can focus on – until he hears Paul's voice.

"Patrick! Can you relax – a little – please?"

The others are startled by the rebuke, and they look at Patrick. First at his embarrassed down turned face, and then lower at the real reason for Paul's outburst – Patrick's cock is fully erect and pointing straight up.

Patrick is the first to laugh after he mutters, "Oops." Randy and Jason break down, unable to continue holding Dawn above their heads any longer. As Dawn is lowered to the ground, everyone joins in Patrick's laughter. Even Paul laughs, knowing the shoot is over, but satisfied that he has succeeded in capturing his vision – as well as some unusually candid photos to share with the models.

"Thank you everyone!" Paul declares. "I'm not sure what happened at the end there, but you all did a wonderful job. You may now go and wash off all of the paint."

The models respond with equal gratitude to Paul's praise as each of them receive a a warm, white bathrobe to wear on their way to the shower. Jason, Randy and Patrick head out right away, having spent quite enough time as trees, but Paul asks Dawn to stay behind so that he can take some photos of her lying in the leaves. It sounds like a great idea, and Dawn is more than willing to help out Paul with a few extra shots. Dawn lies in the leaves, and as she had suspected, she blends right in, almost disappearing. Only her hair and face are still clearly visible as she hides her unpainted hands in the leaves.

Dawn poses provocatively on the bed of red and gold, spurred on by thoughts of Jason's fingers playing between her legs. For a moment, Paul is unable to take a picture, mesmerized by the image he's viewing through the lens. Eventually, Dawn hears the click of the camera shutter, and the flash of the lights pierces her closed eyelids. Again and again come the flashes in quick succession, and Dawn loses track of the number of photos being snapped. Then it all stops, and there is silence. Dawn opens her eyes to see Paul's outstretched hand offered in support. She reaches up and Paul helps her to her feet.

"You are perfect Dawn." Paul smiles gently and nods, closing his eyes and almost bowing. "Thank you so much. Now go wash off that paint."

"Thank you, Paul." Dawn kisses him softly on the cheek, then she throws on the bathrobe, grabs her bag and purse, and heads to the shower.

8:37 PM

Dawn walks along the hallway to the stairs and descends one level. She heads down the next long corridor to the shower, fully expecting to pass the guys on their way back to the studio. As she nears the showers, there is still no sign of the others. Entering the changing room for the shower she notices three bathrobes hung on hooks, and hears Jason's voice through the sound of running water.

"This shit doesn't wash off as easy as they said it would!"

"I know!" Randy replies. "The black lines are the worst."

Dawn removes her bathrobe, hanging it on a hook, and throws her bag and purse on one of the benches lining the walls, before stepping through the doorway to the showers. There are five shower heads in the tiled room – one on the left wall – three on the wall facing her – one on the right wall.

Three of the five shower heads are spraying water over the naked bodies of the men she has just been posing with. Randy is under the one to the left. Jason stands under the middle shower directly in front of Dawn. Patrick is using the shower on the right wall. They've managed to keep as much space between them as possible, Dawn notices with a smirk on her face. Most of the body paint is washed from the men's bodies, but they are still scrubbing at some of the darker lines that won't quite go away, and they don't notice Dawn entering. Not until she attracts their attention.

"You guys are still in here?" She asks jokingly. "I hope you don't mind if I join you, I can't wait all night."

"I don't think you'll hear any complaints from us," Jason jokes back.

"It takes a bit to get all of this paint off," Patrick adds.

"You guys might have to help me then," Dawn teases, as she walks in, choosing the shower between Jason and Patrick. She turns on the water and allows the warm spray to start it's work of removing the body paint. Rubbing her hands over her body as the paint runs off, Dawn seeks to calm the grumbling of the men, and directs her attention to Patrick.

"So what happened?" She asks.

"What do you mean?" Patrick responds.

"During the shoot. Near the end." Dawn keeps prying. "What got you all excited?"

"The view." Patrick states matter-of-factly. "You know I could see everything."

"Everything?"

"I could see right between your legs." Jason, hiding a smile, looks down at the shower floor as Dawn looks at him with a smile of her own. Dawn was pretty sure that Patrick's sudden erection during the shoot occurred because he could see what Jason was doing to her, but she was hoping Patrick would confirm it in front of everyone.

Randy chimes in, "Better view than I had. All I saw during the shoot was Dawn's hair and her back. You've got a great back Dawn – but still."

"It wasn't just the view of Dawn," Patrick continues. "I could see what Jason was doing to her as well."

A confused look clouds Randy's face, an obvious indication that he has no idea what transpired to cause the complete break down of the photo shoot.

"Wait a minute," He injects. "What was Jason doing that I missed?"

"I'm not saying," Patrick replies. "Ask Jason."

"Jason?" Randy turns to him looking for an answer.

Suddenly much more shy, Jason concentrates on looking down at his feet. Now being put on the spot, he appears to have lost his bravado.

Getting nowhere with Jason, Randy asks Dawn, "What was he doing to you?"

Jason doesn't give Dawn the opportunity of answering the question. Looking to Randy, he spits out one word, "Nothing."

Dawn holds her head under the shower, and lets the water pour over her. "Come on Jason – it was more than nothing."

Jason just shakes his head and laughs, "Well I'm not saying anything."

Dawn, turning her bum toward Jason, teases, "You don't have to say anything. Show Randy what you were doing."

Patrick laughs at Dawn's suggestion, but turns to watch, just in case Jason actually goes through with it and shows Randy.

"What did he do?" Randy impatiently pushes for an answer. "Did he pinch your ass or something?"

"Something." Dawn winks, her bum still turned in Jason's direction.

"Definitely something." Patrick continues to laugh, pleased that the attention is no longer on him and his photo shoot erection.

"C'mon, somebody tell me or show me!" Randy is practically begging now.

"I'll show you!" Patrick offers.

Dawn looks at Patrick. "No." And then looks back at Jason. "Jason did it – he should be the one."

Dawn, being so open and encouraging, is restoring Jason's courage. A smile appears on his face, and he shakes his head, preparing to play along. Without saying a word he approaches Dawn from behind, places his one hand on her butt cheek and wraps his fingers between her legs, slightly touching her pussy.

"I just put my hand like this as I was holding her up," Jason finally confesses.

"You were doing more than just holding her up," Patrick mutters.

"Yeah," Dawn adds. "I seem to remember a little more than that."

Jason looks at Dawn's smile and shakes his head again. "You really want me to get into all of the details?" he asks.

"Sure," Dawn replies. "Randy was a part of the shoot too. He should know what was really going on. Besides, it was just getting good right before everyone started laughing, and Paul ended things."

Jason reacts positively to Dawn's assertion that it was getting good – she actually had enjoyed his touch, and now she wants him to touch her again – as much as he wants to touch her. He reaches down and lifts her left leg, pulling her ankle to his chest, which forces her to lean sideways, toward the wall. The sudden repositioning catches Dawn off guard and she exhales deeply as her cheek and hands press against the cold tiles.

With Dawn's one foot firmly planted on the wet floor and the other held against Jason's chest, Randy and Patrick get a full view of Jason's intended target. Jason reaches toward Dawn and uses his hand to wash away the final remnants of paint from between her legs. That alone sends shivers through Dawn's body, and she watches as the paint runs away, with the water, revealing her newly shaved pussy. Being so exposed to the three men, and having them staring so intently, gives her a sudden rush, and her delight is amplified. What started as a tease has turned into intense sexual arousal and Dawn waits anxiously for another touch from Jason's fingers.

From this angle, Jason is unable to hold Dawn's butt cheek as he had before, so he simply places his fingers over her pussy. He begins to rub her clit with his forefinger and then gently slides his middle finger into her pussy. Dawn closes her eyes and delicately bites down on her bottom lip. The knowledge that Randy and Patrick are watching as Jason penetrates her with his finger and caresses her clit, heightens her sensitivity to the touch, and she starts moving against Jason's hand, but he begins to pull his hand away. Interested in continuing, yet content that he has fulfilled Dawn's request to show Randy what had developed during the photo shoot, Jason believes that Dawn is satisfied – her urging tells him differently.

"Don't stop!"

Dawn opens her eyes and looks at Jason.

"Don't stop," She repeats softly.

Jason looks at Dawn and the two of them lock eyes. Slowly, Jason moves his hand back to Dawn's pussy, and he begins caressing her clit once again. He watches her face for a reaction as he re-inserts his finger into her pussy. Dawn closes her eyes again, and whispers, "Yes," as she resumes moving her hips and pressing against Jason's hand.

Still leaning against the wall for support Dawn opens her eyes in the direction of Patrick, who has moved a little closer, with his erect cock pointing straight up to the ceiling, just as it was when Paul had told him to relax. Dawn doesn't react in the same manner. Her reaction is quite the opposite and she stretches out her right arm. Glorifying in Patrick's hardness, she opens her hand wide, motioning for him to come closer. Hesitant at first, Patrick finally approaches, walking his cock right into Dawn's pleading hand.

Dawn closes her hand around the erection, gently pulling it in her direction. Now near to her, Dawn rubs the head of Patrick's cock against her cheek and strokes his straight length. Admiring the intensity of the rock hard shaft in her hand, Dawn licks it's fullness from balls to head, then flicks her tongue across the tip, continuing the full handed strokes. The added excitement of having Patrick join in has Dawn breathing heavier and moaning tenderly as her eyes peer over in Randy's direction.

Randy is still standing under the shower, intensely watching the threesome in the corner. Dawn notices that Randy's penis is only now beginning to harden. Perhaps it's the unexpected attention that she's giving him, but as she looks on, he stiffens and grows. Seeing Randy's arousal in motion, Dawn pushes harder against Jason's hand and begins to stroke Patrick with added vigor. Randy is fully erect now and Dawn adores the sight of the cock's swollen head resting atop of the upward curved shaft. Her smile of approval entices Randy and he approaches the threesome, obviously intent on receiving some of her attention. She watches as he nears and is overwhelmed by the idea of having all three of the men close and touching her.

Patrick has begun massaging Dawn's breasts, and she doesn't notice him staring down at her hand as she works on his cock – her gaze is on Randy as he kneels down by her, placing one hand on each of her thighs, and looking directly at her pussy. She becomes acutely aware that she has drawn the attention of three ferociously strong males and her heart skips as she views the intensity in Randy's eyes.

Jason pulls his hand away from Dawn's pussy and slides it across her body, finding his way to her chest. She tilts her head back as Jason takes charge of her right breast while Patrick focuses on her left – and then she feels Randy's tongue touch her pussy. She shivers as Randy slips his tongue inside of her and then upward toward her clit where he begins to flick it rapidly. The sensation causes her to tremble and shudder, and she is surprised by how quickly she feels herself nearing orgasm. She places her mouth on the bottom of Patrick's cock and rubs the shaft and head between her lips in time with her hand. She can hear herself getting louder in response to all of the stimuli as Randy moves a finger into her pussy – and another calmly into her bum.

Dawn feels the start of her orgasm as Patrick begins groaning and thrusting his hips in time with Dawn's treatment of his cock. They both cum simultaneously. Dawn's screams of pleasure echo off the tiled walls as she pushes against Randy's fingers and tongue. Patrick's cum shoots across Dawn's cheek, and she grips his cock harder as their mutual climaxes reach a peek.

Patrick pulls away and sinks to the floor, sighing. Dawn's orgasm hasn't tired her, but instead, has ignited her passion, and she pulls away from Randy and Jason's grip. Dawn drops to the floor and turns, for the first time seeing Jason's fully erect cock. For a moment, she is caught off guard by its impressive size, stretching straight forward as if weighed down by its own mass. So long and wide – Dawn has never been with a man of such vast extent. Dawn crawls past Jason's tremendous cock, brushing the side of her face against it momentarily as she moves toward the goal she has in mind – to please Randy in the same way that he has just pleased her.

Randy is sitting on the floor and Dawn moves forcefully toward him, pushing him onto his back. Completely overcome with the passion of the moment, Dawn now desires to have Randy's cock in her mouth more than any other before. She positions herself between his legs, and without pause, plunges his cock past her lips and to the back of her tongue. Randy is startled by the sudden attack, and overpowered by the pleasure of having his cock so deeply in Dawn's mouth, he falls back, holding his head and staring straight up at the ceiling. With one hand gripping Randy's shaft and the other massaging his balls, Dawn devours his cock. Her knees on the ground and her hips in the air, she sways back and forth, enticing Jason to move. She isn't sure what to expect, or if she will even be able to handle the size, but she knows that she needs Jason's cock inside her pussy as severely as she needs Randy's cock in her mouth.

Dawn waits for Jason while focusing on pleasing Randy, who is now writhing on the floor and lifting his hips off of the ground. Dawn feels her pussy opening under the pressure of the head of Jason's cock. Pausing from sucking Randy's cock, Dawn prepares for what she believes will be too much of Jason for her to handle, as she feels him gripping her hips. But Jason's entry is paced and gentle. First, just the head and then he pulls back. With the next move forward, Jason submerges another inch of his massive cock into Dawn, examining her reaction as he does. And again he pulls back. Dawn is moved by Jason's attention to her comfort as he considerately progresses deeper with each push, allowing her muscles to relax and openly receive him.

Dawn looks at Randy and then down at her hand still stroking his cock. Leaning forward again she places her mouth over his cock, and closes her lips around the base of the head. Sucking the tip, she deeply massages the front with her tongue. At the same time, she feels Jason press forward again, and with this next thrust, the full length of his cock plunges deep inside her.

Dawn works vigorously on Randy's cock as Jason begins the motion of easing in and out of her, allowing her to feel the length and width of his cock with each long stroke. Patrick looks on, his erection quickly reappearing, and Dawn looks over at him as his cock grows to it's full stature again, and the visual adds to the moment. Dawn's sounds of pleasure grow louder as she hears both Randy and Jason express their delight. Jason starts to take slower, more powerful strokes. Dawn forces as much of Randy's cock into her mouth as she possibly can and holds it there, her muffled moans vibrating against the head. Randy breathes deep, and with a loud groan cum pours from the tip of his cock. Jason, emulating Randy's sounds pushes all of the way into Dawn as his cum begins filling her pussy. As quickly as Randy's cum enters Dawn's open mouth, she allows it to flow back out, massaging it up and down over his cock. The warmth of Jason's orgasm hits Dawn deep in her pussy as she feels him throb and jerk inside of her. Dawn's second orgasm comes on faster and stronger than her first. Unable to control her response, her moans grow into screams with each wave of her orgasm, begging for this to go on forever.

Her head spinning, Dawn rolls over onto her back under the still streaming shower heads. The moment seems surreal as she looks around at the three men sitting on the floor around her. She carefully stands up and walks over to the center shower head. As she closes her eyes and tilts her head back under the water, she suddenly feels the touch of hands. One hand at first, then three, and finally six hands caressing and exploring her body. Dawn opens her eyes to the men, reaching out and touching them in return. Right in front of her, stands Patrick, and she kisses him first. A gentle kiss with their tongues meeting at the edge of their lips. Then she turns to Randy on her left, and opens her mouth as he leans forward, and they begin kissing – Randy's mouth, as adept at pleasing her mouth as it was at pleasing her pussy. As she feels Jason's hand approach her right breast, she turns to him, and kisses him – her mouth inviting his tongue inside with the same enthusiasm as her pussy had invited his cock.

The four of them stand under the water. The men run their hands over Dawn's body, each of them taking turns kissing her neck and breasts – touching her pussy and massaging her clit. One by one, fingers enter and exit her pussy, and she loses track of which digit belongs to which of the adoring men. Hands reach behind and grasp her bum, and a finger probes the valley between her cheeks, looking for the entrance. It must be Randy, Dawn thinks, identifying the owner of the finger that finds it's way into her tight hole. Each of the men has been so attentive to Dawn – her response – her pleasure – her comfort – she freely gives in to the exploration.

In turn, Dawn explores with her hands, the smooth bodies that surround her. She runs her hands over Patrick's chest and reaches down, discovering that he is still hard. With both hands, she holds his cock, while at the same time, she feels a new finger enter her pussy – shortly followed by a gentle push forward of the finger in her bum. She searches with her hands, finding Randy and

Jason's soft penises and massages them until she feels them growing stiff in her hands.

It doesn't take long for the hands of three men to bring Dawn close to another orgasm. Her body begins to jerk, as Randy's finger finds it's way deeper into her bum, gently massaging along the way. Randy and Jason each have a finger inside her pussy and she grips their now hard cocks as Patrick vigorously tickles her clit. The wave after wave of intense pleasure that pounds Dawn's body, is so overwhelming that she is unable to utter a sound – until the final, most powerful wave forces her to cry out in ecstasy.

Dawn's body falls limp, and the men help her to the floor, where she slides her bum across the wet tiles and finds the corner with her back. Looking up she views Jason, Patrick and Randy, standing a few feet away, their cocks fully erect and straining for release. The sight brings Dawn's weakened body to life once more, knowing that she will not be totally satisfied until each of the men are as complete as her. With outreached hands and her mouth agape, she motions for them to come closer.

Jason is the first to respond, and he walks up to Dawn as she makes her way to her knees. As soon as Jason is within reach, Dawn grabs a hold of his excessive cock with both hands, pulls him in, and passes the enormous head through her lips. Not much more than the head will fit into her mouth, but she holds it there, working on it with her tongue and sucking the tip. Using both hands, she jerks Jason's cock so hard that he must move his hips to keep up with the motion.

Dawn notices that Randy and Patrick have taken up positions on either side of her, and she eyes their hard and begging cocks. Keeping Jason in her mouth, she reaches out and grabs Randy's erection to her right and Patrick's to her left. She moves her mouth over the head of Jason's cock, not wanting to let go, but desperately wanting to please the other two men who have brought her so much pleasure. Finally, releasing the head of Jason's cock, Dawn turns her lips toward Randy, and takes the familiar curve of his cock deep into her mouth as eagerly as she had earlier.

Patrick's cock seems to grow harder in Dawn's hand as he watches her milk Randy with her other hand and mouth. Taking notice and wanting to give equal attention to all, Dawn slides her mouth, but not her hand, off of Randy's cock. She continues to stroke Randy as she transitions to Patrick's much straighter, and amazingly hard erection. She pauses in the middle to momentarily take Jason into her mouth once again, looking up into his eyes as she savors the head of his cock. But Patrick's cock is throbbing in Dawn's left hand, begging to be sucked, and she is not about to disappoint any of her attentive lovers.

Patrick's slender cock stands straight up, and Dawn has to pull against the force of the erection in order to point the tip towards her mouth. Looking up at Patrick, Dawn pauses for a moment, holding the head of his cock against her lips, teasing the tip with her tongue. Patrick breaks under the pressure and pushes his hips forward, and the head of his cock disappears into Dawn's mouth, causing her eyes to widen with surprise at the sudden intrusion. Patrick stops himself, fearing that he has become too aggressive and possibly taken advantage of Dawn's generosity. He attempts to pull back, but Dawn has reached behind him and has her hand on his bum, holding him in place. She stares directly into his eyes as she pushes forward, forcing his cock into her mouth and to the edge of her throat.

The force of the action and the intensity of the sensation causes Patrick to throw back his head as he reaches down and grabs a hold of Dawn's hair. Instinctively, he struggles to gain control of the situation, but Dawn refuses to relinquish the upper hand. She holds his ass firmly as she massages the head of his cock with the back of her tongue while licking his balls with the tip. Patrick's body quakes as he groans deeply, and Dawn pulls back, allowing his erection to spring from her mouth. A stream of cum bursts from Patrick's cock, streaking Dawn's upper lip and cheek, and the force of his erection points his cock straight up to the ceiling once again. Dawn releases Patrick's ass and grabs onto the flexing cock, massaging it and drawing out more cum, catching some on her tongue and allowing the rest to run over her fingers until Patrick can take no more, fading backward to rest on the floor, utterly spent.

Enthralled by Patrick's reaction, Dawn watches him slink away as she wipes his cum from her cheek, but she hasn't forgotten about the two men that remain standing, and she has continued jerking Randy's cock while attending to Patrick. And now, with her unoccupied left hand, she finds Jason's balls and she cups them in her palm while turning to Randy. She begins to jerk Randy's cock rapidly, only slowing occasionally to lick the tip and encircle the head with her tongue. Randy places his hand on the wall behind Dawn, and hunches over as his hips start shaking. Dawn glances into Randy's eyes before returning her stare to the tip of his cock, waiting for the flow of cum that quickly approaches. She feels Randy's shaft swell in her hand as he lets out an agonizing cry, and braces himself against the wall and her shoulder. The rush of cum explodes from Randy's cock, showering her breasts, and she leans in to catch each drop, and then uses her tongue to coax the last of it from the tip. Breathless and shaking, Randy pulls away and drops to the floor.

Jason is the last man standing, his balls still cupped by Dawn's hand – his cock stiffened to it's limit as he watches her smooth Randy's cum over her breasts. And then she looks up at him, ready to give him her full attention. He bends over and softly kisses her cheek, then slowly straightens up, smiling and gazing into her eyes. With both hands, Dawn grips Jason's cock firmly, taking the time to examine it closely as she moves her mouth to it. As she squeezes the head past her lips, the awareness that she has an audience in Patrick and Randy drives her passion, and she attacks Jason's throbbing cock, her hands working the shaft while her mouth devours the head. It isn't long before Jason lets out a series of short grunts and Dawn feels his cum filling her mouth. She pulls away long enough to swallow, before taking the head back in, kneading Jason's cock with both hands, and sucking every last bit of cum into her mouth and down her throat.

Jason pounds the wall with his fist as Dawn carefully drains him, purposely swallowing hard, letting him know that not a drop is going to waste. When Jason finally pulls back, he doesn't drop to the floor as the others did, but instead takes a step back to catch his breath. He looks at Dawn for a moment, and then steps forward, reaching out to clasp her hands and guiding her to her feet. He walks her over to a shower and places her under the streaming water. As Randy and Patrick stand up from their places on the floor and return to their showers to wash off the last remnants of body paint that still spot their bodies, Jason washes Dawn's body with his hands, gently caressing every inch – his eyes following his hands closely – admiringly. Dawn holds her hands above her head with her eyes closed, relishing Jason's caring touch, and she hears him whisper in her ear.

"We should work together again some time."

"Yes we should," Dawn whispers back. "And maybe hang out a little after the shoot again."

"I like the sound of that." Jason smiles.

"Will you bring some friends?" Dawn asks coyly.

Jason's smile broadens and becomes a laugh. "I'll tell Paul to give you my number."

Randy shuts off the water from his shower. "Well, I'm all done."

"Yeah, same here," Patrick says as he too shuts of his water.

Jason steps back from Dawn as Randy walks over to them. Dawn reaches out to Randy for a hug, and he walks into her open arms.

"You are amazing Dawn," Randy says, hugging Dawn.

"Yes you are," Patrick adds, stepping up to Dawn, kissing her on the cheek and getting a hug in return.

"How do I respond to that?" Dawn asks, genuinely moved by what she's just experienced. "Thank you for an amazing time!"

No one is quite sure how to respond or move beyond the moment. And so, after a few friendly goodbyes, Randy and Patrick exit, leaving Dawn and Jason alone in the shower.

"I hope I'll see you again," Jason tells Dawn.

"I'll get your number from Paul," Dawn responds.

Jason gives Dawn a quick peck on the cheek and turns, walking away. Dawn watches Jason's magnificent physique, and cute bum, slowly stroll across the floor toward the doorway.

"Jason!" Dawn calls out.

Jason turns and looks at Dawn, waiting to see if she has more to say than just his name. He doesn't wait long before hearing the invitation, "Kiss me."

Jason doesn't move, so Dawn repeats, "Kiss me. Kiss me like you've wanted to all evening."

Jason walks back toward Dawn, his slow, deliberate steps, sending shivers up her spine. Dawn lowers her head slightly as Jason approaches, and they wrap their arms around each other. Jason tilts his head, touching his forehead against Dawn's. The seconds pass, and then Dawn lifts her head, looking up at Jason and biting her lower lip softly. Jason moves his mouth toward her's, and her eyes open wide as their lips touch, then close tight as their tongues meet. Jason's kiss is powerful, yet soft, and Dawn responds in like. They hold each other firmly, not wanting the other person to escape the embrace of the kiss. The end of the kiss is as tender as the start, and finishes with them both pulling back to look at each other.

Almost simultaneously, Dawn breathes the

words, "I'll call you", as Jason utters, "Call me." The two of them allow their arms to fall away from the embrace, and Jason steps back, finally turning away and hesitantly leaving. Dawn watches until Jason disappears into the change room, then listens for the door to close behind him as he exits.

Dawn pieces together the events of the evening and relives them in her mind as she finishes showering, before moving to the change room to blow dry her hair and fix her make-up. Putting her jean skirt and tank top on, she grabs her bag and purse, and walks out into the hallway. The halls are quiet as she makes her way through the building. She pulls out her phone and calls the usual cab company as she walks. Back in the lobby, Dawn peers through the glass doors at the front of the building, looking out at the darkness, waiting for her cab.

9:28 PM

Summer is coming to a close and autumn is quickly approaching. A light rain has started to fall, and Dawn feels a chill in the night air as she steps outside. The cab seems to be taking it's time, and Dawn has decided to take a look up and down the street to see if maybe the taxi is at one of the other entrances to the building. Just then a brand new black sports car pulls up to the curb. The car doesn't look familiar to Dawn, and she takes a step back toward the door of the building, trying to get a view of the driver through the cars tinted windows. The driver's window lowers and instantly Dawn recognizes the face, which puzzles her.

"Waiting for a ride?" the driver asks with a smile. "You can't trust those damn cab companies to show up on time."

"Umm?" Dawn questions. "This doesn't look like the car you were driving this morning."

"That wasn't mine."

"Did you borrow it or steal it?"

"No, I own it – I just don't usually drive it."

"So, you own a cab that you don't drive?"

"Something like that."

"Do you own this car?"

"I do."

"Do you *usually* drive it?"

"Yes, I do."

"You're not making a whole lot of sense."

"I can explain. Let me give you a ride home Dawn, and I can explain."

"And you'll explain how you know my name?"

"Carl told me."

"Carl? How do you know Carl?"

"I can explain."

Dawn walks around to the passenger door and opens it, just as the rain begins to pick up. "Alright – explain." She sits down in the front seat and closes the door. "Before we go anywhere, you need to explain a few things."

"Fair enough," the driver replies.

"You can start with your name since you already know mine."

"Allister."

"Alright Allister, how do you know Carl?"

"Carl worked for me when I first started my business. He was in school and drove one of the first two cabs I owned. We've been friends ever since."

"Wait – so you don't drive for 'ABC Taxi' – you own 'ABC Taxi'?"

"Allister Brady Copeland – ABC made sense. But it's actually 'ABC Car Services'. We also have a limousine service."

"But 'ABC' is the largest cab company in the city."

"One hundred and thirty-seven taxis – plus twenty-three limousines, eight sedans, six Hummer limos, and three limo-buses."

"Are you bragging now?"

"I'm explaining – you asked me to explain."

"Okay, explain to me why the owner of a taxi company asks one of my co-workers for my name – picks me up in a cab this morning – masturbates in that cab in front of me – and then randomly shows up here tonight. How long have you been stalking me?"

"Wait a minute! I haven't stalked you! I've only seen you three times in my life. The first was last Christmas."

"Last Christmas?"

"Well, just before last Christmas – after the KPR Christmas party."

Dawn starts to speak but stops when Allister holds up a finger, and interrupts her, "I'm explaining. May I finish?"

Dawn relents, "Alright, continue."

"As I said before, Carl worked for me when I was just starting the car service. He helped me get my business off the ground. When that pretentious prick Marshal Preston started hiring my company for special events, I made a point of driving Carl for every KPR Christmas party. It gives me a chance to work for him and thank him for all he's done. We just have fun with it."

And then silence – a long moment of silence. Dawn allows a pause to ensure that Allister is finished his explanation, and then blurts out, "I knew I recognized you this morning!"

"Well I definitely recognized you," comes Allister's quick response. "You made a fairly powerful first impression. I asked Carl that night who you were. He was going to introduce us, but I didn't think such a beautiful young lady would give a second thought to an older limo driver."

"But you're not a 'limo driver', you're the owner of the company. How old are you anyway?"

"52."

"I thought something like that."

"You didn't know I owned the company."

"No, I didn't."

"I didn't want you be interested in me because of that, and I guess I didn't have the confidence in myself to think that you'd be interested in me in any other way. Carl told me your name, and that was all. I left it at that. But this morning, I was driving one of our new cabs because I like to take the new cars out for a spin – I don't know why – I just do – I enjoy it – it takes me back. So, I'm driving around and dispatch announces a pick-up, and I'm pretty close – so I decide, what the hell – I'll do it for old times sake. I show up, you walk out, and before I can say anything, you're being all sexy in the backseat and I'm tongue-tied – and of course I'm turned on. And don't forget, it was you that got me to masturbate. I was trying to cover up, but you pulled that little stunt, making me reach for the money. And then..."

"Can you blame me?" Dawn interrupts. "Cab driver, limo driver, rich man – it didn't matter. You had a way about yourself. Attractive, kind of shy, pleasant – and you seemed familiar – I know why now – but I was comfortable with you. Besides, seeing you in your state, how could I not be turned on a little? Honestly, I was quite surprised when you went ahead and jerked off."

"I wish I would have done it all differently."

"You did a pretty good job from what I saw."

"No no, that's not what I mean. I mean..." Allister fumbles with his words, wishing his mouth could express what his mind is thinking and his heart is feeling. "I realized then that I had been foolish in the limo. I should have allowed Carl to introduce us. You have been on my mind since that night. When you just walked away from the cab this morning – before I had a chance to say something – I hated myself for not speaking up. So, I told dispatch to let me know if any calls come in for a pick-up or drop-off at your home address, or your work address. I had to see you again – I had to say something."

The sound of rain drops hitting the roof of the car is all that is heard, as Dawn and Allister sit quietly pondering the things that have been said. Allister stares out the windshield, not sure if he wants to hear Dawn's response to his explanation. Dawn also stares straight ahead, not knowing exactly how to respond. Finally, the silence is broken by the two words that slip from Dawn's lips.

"You're sweet."

And the only reply is the repeating sound of rain drops.

Dawn carries on, "I'm glad you said something."

Allister sits, both hands on the steering wheel, still staring out through the windshield, and Dawn wonders if Allister is glad that he had said something. And again, the only sound is the thrumming beat of droplets hitting the car.

"You know..." Dawn buckles up her seat belt. "I skipped dinner. And after the workout I've just had, I'm starving."

Allister looks over at Dawn and smiles. "I didn't realize there is gym in this building."

"There isn't," Dawn responds. "It's full of studios – mostly art studios – photography to be exact. Carl must have told you that I model."

"He did, but I didn't know that's what you were doing tonight. And I didn't know that modeling was such a workout."

Dawn laughs, knowing what Allister doesn't know about her evening. "I'll have to tell you about it sometime."

"Well, would you like to get a bite to eat?"

"That would be nice. We can chat more. You've intrigued me. I want to know more about you. I'd like to hear more about Allister Brady Copeland."

"I'm afraid you may be bored, but I'll tell you whatever you'd like to know. And I can't wait to hear more about you if you'd care to share," Allister beams.

Throwing the car into gear, Allister pulls away from the curb and sets out to find a quiet spot to grab a bite to eat and converse. Suddenly feeling much more relaxed after driving for a few blocks, Allister opens up with some small talk.

"I've only seen you dressed for the Christmas party and for work," Allister comments, noticing Dawn's tank top and jean skirt. "Always so dressed up – so perfect – but here you are, so casual, and still so perfect. Definitely a different style than this morning."

Dawn thinks of how she was dressed on her way to work, realizing how drastically different her outfit is now. She also remembers all that she showed Allister during their cab ride earlier in the day, and she places her hand in her lap, sneaking a feel of her bald pussy through her skirt. "You have no idea how different I look compared to this morning, when you picked me up in the cab, and watched me through the mirror," Dawn laughs.

"What do you mean?" Allister asks.

Dawn thinks about showing him, but decides against it for now. "I'll explain later," she says with a smirk.

"Sounds like you have a few stories to share," Allister remarks as he pushes a button on the car's stereo. Dawn instantly recognizes Dean Martin singing 'Everybody Loves Somebody'. Hearing the voice stirs her memory of the night in the limo when her and Allister first met – or didn't quite meet – and Dawn's curiosity about this man is heightened. They drive the short distance to a small cafe, listening to the music and saying nothing more. Allister pulls into the parking lot, shuts off the engine, and jumps out to jog through the light rain, around to Dawn's side of the car. Opening the door for her, he takes her hand and helps her out of the vehicle, and continues to hold her hand as they rush into the restaurant. Once inside they order something to eat at the counter and then seek out a quiet corner.

The vacant booth that they find isn't exactly quiet, sitting amongst the crowd in the busy cafe, but neither of them seem bothered by the background noise as each of them focus on the other. As hungry as Dawn is, food doesn't seem to interest her at the moment as she begins opening up to Allister. She starts off by explaining about the night in the back of the limousine, and detailing her relationship with Carl and Beverly. She moves on to talk about her modeling – including the photo shoot that she just finished, not forgetting to add the part about the shaved pussy.

"So that's what you meant about looking so different?" Allister interrupts.

Dawn smiles and nods, "Maybe I'll show you later."

Allister blushes, "I'd like that." He is enthralled by what he's heard so far, and presses Dawn, "Go on, tell me more about you."

"Alright – well..." And Dawn continues by telling Allister about her job, and some of the other things that make up her life – even recounting some of the more risque events of the busy day she's had. The more Dawn talks, the more earnestly Allister listens – and the more Dawn desires to be honest about who she is and the life that she enjoys. Everything that she throws out, Allister receives with interest and acceptance, sometimes asking questions – always encouraging her to reveal more of herself. She can't remember a time when she has felt more relaxed sharing the intimate details of her life. Why him? What is it about this man that has her baring her soul. She feels almost naked sitting there – naked and vulnerable, yet so safe.

Dawn desires deeply to know more of this person that presently has such a firm hold on her. He doesn't disappoint, and with an effortless transition, Allister takes over the lead in the conversation, sharing details of his life – how he's spent most of his time focused on his company – how his relationships have consisted of occasional liaisons and nothing more. Dawn digs deeper with her questions and listens intently to each of Allister's anecdotes. Frequently mesmerized by his charm and eloquence, she finds herself asking him to repeat certain details. He laughs at each request, but happily and diligently recounts each story until Dawn is satisfied that she's ingested every detailed point of what is being shared.

"Dawn," Allister pointedly remarks as the conversation wanes, "you are fascinating."

"Why thank you, Mr. Copeland," Dawn replies with an air of formality, and she feels herself blush. "You are quite fascinating as well."

Allister pauses to collect his thoughts before hesitantly continuing, "With your day job and your modeling – and all of your friends and acquaintances – would it be possible for you to find the time for us to spend some time together – get to know each other better?"

"Well if I can tear you away from running your business," Dawn teases. "I think that I would enjoy getting closer to you as well."

"I believe it's time I learned to invest in more important things than my business," Allister remarks as he stands. "But for now, I should probably get you home."

Dawn stands. "Yes, we should get going." And as she walks past Allister she adds. "Besides, I have something I'd like to show you."

10:15 PM

The sky has opened up, and the rain pours down over the empty parking lot. Allister wishes that there had been a closer parking spot available when they arrived earlier as he and Dawn run to the car, which is sitting in the shadows, just out of reach of the lone light shining dimly overhead. Allister reaches the passenger side door first, opening it and guiding Dawn into the seat, before slamming the door and running around to the driver's side. Allister hops in behind the wheel and pulls the door closed quickly as he slips the key into the ignition, giving it a turn, causing the interior light to shut off and the dash to light up. The engine roars to life and Allister reaches up to turn the interior light back on.

"Let me get the heat going," Allister says as he looks over to Dawn. "You must be freezing."

"It is a little chilly," Dawn responds. "I'm soaked!"

Allister just sits there and stares at Dawn. Her hair is drenched, and water drips down over her face. The t-shirt she is wearing clings to her wet body, her nipples firm from the cold and visible through the material. She kicks off her soggy shoes as she rubs her legs, pushing the water off of them, and trying to warm her goose-bump covered limbs.

"Let's get you home," Allister suggests, grabbing the gear shift.

Dawn stops him. "Not yet. Let's let the car warm up a bit first."

"Alright," Allister agrees, taking his hand from the gear shift and rubbing his biceps for warmth, he looks out the windshield at the downpour.

"I want to show you something." Dawn's voice is barely heard over the sound of the pouring rain beating against the sports car's roof. Allister looks over at Dawn just as she starts to lift her skirt. "What do you think?" She asks, slowly revealing the area where her landing strip used to be.

"Wow!" Allister reacts. "You really did shave it off. What can I say? You look as amazing as ever."

"I think I'll miss my stripe," Dawn confides, gently rubbing the area with her finger. "I'll probably let it grow back. Maybe I'll change up the design. I think I'd like to try a little triangle or something."

"I've only seen the stripe a couple of times – it looked good on you. A triangle will probably look good too. Anything would look good on you."

"Well, I'll have to grow it back and you can have a better look at it, then tell me what you think."

"I hope to be around long enough for that," Allister manages to say as he watches closely at Dawn continuing to stroke the area.

"I think you will be," Dawn tells Allister, looking up at him, and noticing his eyes fixed on her pussy. "But in the meantime, we can enjoy it just like it is. Might as well have some fun with it."

Allister doesn't say a word but only watches as Dawn turns in her seat, leaning against the door and raising her left foot to his shoulder. The car's engine suddenly roars as Allister's foot unexpectedly presses down on the accelerator. Moving his foot and burying his face in the steering wheel, he apologizes as the engine calms down, "Sorry about that. My foot must have slipped."

"You are so cute!" Dawn laughs.

Allister smiles, lifting his head and looking back at Dawn. "Thanks."

Dawn winks, slowly moving her hand down and lifting her skirt, revealing her glistening pussy. Allister swallows with a gulp – his reaction exciting Dawn as she holds her skirt up with her left hand, her right hand bashfully covering her pussy. She spreads her fingers slightly, leaving her middle finger resting directly over the divide. With Allister's eyes fixed between her legs, she presses with her middle finger, sliding it into her pussy. Her own reaction is not a planned part of the display, but a reflection of her heightened arousal at putting on a show for such a keen audience. Her hips arch and the air leaves her lungs in a loud gasp as she closes her eyes. Her finger moves in and out of her pussy as her bum leaves the seat. The intensity rises as she slips her finger over her clit, at first massaging it slowly, and then allowing the speed to progress.

Using her free hand, Dawn lifts her wet t-shirt, baring her breasts, the nipples hard from the chill and arousal. Grabbing her breasts, she arches her back further, her bum rises higher, and her hips buck faster and stronger. Her tongue licks her lips as she massages her breasts, occasionally opening her eyes to watch Allister's reaction. Short bursts of sound rise from her throat as she brings herself nearer and nearer to orgasm. She strains against the pleasure of her own hand, almost as if fighting for control, but eventually releasing and allowing the orgasm to overpower her.

There hasn't been a fantasy person racing through Dawn's thoughts as she masturbates this time. She realizes that the only person that has been on her mind the whole time is Allister, and she opens her eyes once more, to see him watching her orgasm. He appears to be holding his breath as his eyes comb her body. She closes her eyes again – relaxing – fully succumbing to the pleasure. The entire car shakes to the rhythm of Dawn's undulating body, and not even the pounding of the rain against the vehicle's exterior is able to drown out her ecstatic expressions.

And then silence – motionless silence.

Dawn lies still for a moment, recovering from the experience, the sound of the falling rain now relaxing and soothing. Allister is unable to look away, still absorbing the sudden impact of Dawn's orgasm – attempting to correlate that with the quiet, gentle creature that reclines beside him. He remains silent as Dawn sits up straight in her seat, adjusting her skirt and pulling down her t-shirt. It is obvious to Dawn that Allister is not prepared to speak, or perhaps incapable of the simple task of stringing together words to form a sentence, so she leans over and kisses him on the cheek. Allister looks into Dawn's eyes as she pulls back, and four quiet words slip from his lips, "You are amazing, Dawn."

Dawn giggles and repeats her earlier compliment, "You are so cute." Then she kisses Allister on the cheek again, and whispers in his ear, "Can I have that ride home now?"

Allister's only response is a smile as he puts the car into gear, and races away. A few minutes after leaving the parking lot, Dawn and Allister begin to chat again – and they chat all of the way to Dawn's home. This time the conversation doesn't reveal any deep dark secrets, but instead carries on in a relaxed manner, as if the two have been acquaintances for years. The minutes pass quickly by, and before long Allister is pulling the car up in front of Dawn's building, and into a parking space designated for visitors. Dawn unbuckles her seat belt and leans over to kiss Allister, but this time she passes on the cheek, turning his face to hers, and their lips touch. Holding one another, they share their first real kiss – an impassioned kiss that says more than either of them have been able to verbalize all evening. Time and place are forgotten for a few brief moments as they embrace, delighting in the kiss and entranced by each others company.

11:06 PM

      Dawn lays her head back against the edge of the tub as she soaks in the warm water, surrounded by bubbles. Bubble baths are a luxury that she doesn't have the opportunity to enjoy very often with her busy schedule, but after this long day, she is making time. Candles flicker, projecting shimmering lights throughout the small washroom. Louis Armstrong serenades Dawn from the stereo by the sink with 'What a Wonderful World', as she lies silently agreeing. Wonderful indeed – and at the moment when Satchmo carries his last throaty note of the song, she stands up and pushes the lever releasing the bathtub stopper. The water gurgles as it drains and she grabs a towel, wiping the bubbles from her body and patting herself dry. She turns to the stereo, shutting it off before the next song begins to fully form and drag her back into her meditative state. Blowing out the candles, she wraps herself in the towel before heading to the oasis of her bedroom.

When Dawn opens the door, she finds Allister in place. He has done as he was told, and made himself comfortable while Dawn took her bath. Quite comfortable indeed – Allister is sitting up in bed with pillows propped behind his back – a sheet covering his lower body – holding one of Dawn's magazines in one hand and gently petting her cat with the other. He looks up as Dawn enters and asks, "Enjoy your bath?"

"I did," Dawn responds. "I needed that."

Allister puts down the magazine as Dawn walks over and picks up her cat from the bed. Rubbing the purring kitty behind the ears, Dawn carries her to the bedroom door and places her on the floor in the hallway.

"I see Cleo has taken a liking to you," Dawn remarks.

"She just hopped up here and laid down," Allister responds. "I'm guessing she loves attention."

"Very much so," Dawn agrees. "But it's my turn for some attention."

Dropping the towel, Dawn presents her naked body to Allister, turning in circles a couple of times to give him the full view. This brings a smile to Allister's face, and Dawn laughs into her hands playfully, suddenly feeling giddy and full of energy. She strolls to the side of the bed and runs her hand along the form of Allister's leg hidden beneath the sheet. She saunters deliberately toward the head of the bed, tracing Allister's form with her hand as she progresses. She pauses when she reaches his hip, her hand lying within inches of the stiffening form pressing up against the sheet. She moves her hand over the hardness and lightly caresses it as it grows and quivers to her touch until reaching it's full size and strength.

Dawn reaches up and grabs the top of the sheet, throwing it back, and exposing the view that she had been longing for. Allister lay there completely nude, and Dawn takes her time to look over every inch of his sleek body. Her eyes trace across Allister's chest and torso, making their way to his waist and hips. As she had imagined, Allister is carefully groomed from head to toe, with only the shadow of a triangle of closely trimmed hair directing her eyes to the beautiful, erect cock she remembers from this morning.

Dawn sits on the bed, sliding her hand over Allister – admiring every feature of his trim body. She reclines beside him, stretching out her body and intertwining her legs with his. Allister wraps his arms around Dawn, pulling her in and meeting her lips with his own. The memory of Allister pleasuring himself in the front seat of the cab early this morning runs through Dawn's mind, and she reacts the way she had desired to at the time, grabbing a hold of Allister's cock and masturbating it vigorously. Allister releases a deep moan and caresses Dawn's back as he reaches for her breasts, gently kneading and massaging each of them. Then, fulfilling one of his deepest desires, he pulls away from the kiss to allow his mouth to explore Dawn's nipples.

Allister's passion has Dawn reeling, and she grabs his head, pushing his mouth against her breasts while gripping his cock firmly. Dawn looks down at her hand jerking Allister's fully engorged cock, with it's shimmering tip and swollen head. The sight is too much for her to ignore and she pulls away from Allister's embrace, pulling herself toward his cock and taking as much of it as possible, into her mouth. Her hand, which was only moments before gripping and stroking Allister's cock, now kneads his balls earnestly.

Allister's hands grasp at Dawn's breasts as they slip out of reach, and he succumbs to her oral attack. Eventually he admits defeat and places his hands on Dawn's shoulders as her tongue licks slowly down his shaft. As Dawn holds Allister's balls in her hand, she takes one after the other into her mouth, pulling with her lips and tickling with her tongue. Allister throws his head back as Dawn's tongue dances around his balls, and her hand satisfies his cock.

Dawn's pace slows as her want increases. Holding Allister's cock with an open hand, she begins to lick the full length, her eyes now fixed and observing the facial expressions and movements of Allister. She moves up and hovers over him, before laying her body down on his, and looking him in the eyes. For a moment, everything stands still, and then as if in slow motion, Dawn kisses Allister. Lips parted and tongues entwined, their chests pressed tightly together, Allister runs his hands down Dawn's body and holds her bottom firmly. Dawn moves her hips, positioning her pussy on the tip of Allister's cock. She rubs her pussy against the yearning head, wetting them both.

As their bodies move in unison, Allister enters Dawn. She eagerly welcomes him in, pressing down forcefully to accept his all. With that one motion, Allister is almost fully inside of her, and she pushes harder down on him until the head of his cock reaches it's limit deep inside of her. Dawn gasps, discovering that at that limit is a hidden place that elicits tremors throughout her body, as shivers run up her spine and her limbs numb. Allister's cock has found a place that even Dawn herself didn't know about, and her reaction to the contact is immediate.

"Oh my god!" Dawn screams.

Pleasantly startled, Allister holds Dawn tightly and thrusts his hips upward, again and again as the tip of his cock seeks the spot that makes her respond in such a way. Dawn, in turn, thrusts her pussy down onto Allister's cock as it finds that spot again and again. As their bodies move in rhythmic harmony, Allister rolls Dawn over and lies on top of her. His thrusts are slow and deliberate as he shares in Dawn's pleasure. Dawn lifts her legs off of the bed, wrapping her calves around Allister's lower back – she pulls as he pushes. The shaft of Allister's cock rubs Dawn's clit as they move in concert with one another, the head of his cock endlessly thrilling the spot deep inside of her. Dawn is now repeating, her earlier statement over and over in short breaths, with each of Allister's thrusts.

"Oh my god, oh my god, oh my god!" Dawn cries out, and she pleads for more of her lover's attention. "Please Allister, please!"

Allister's throat closes around his words and his response becomes nothing more than strained expressions of Dawn's name, repeated in time with each forward thrust. Their breaths synchronize with the movement of their bodies, and the rush that floods Dawn's head blurs her senses. Her orgasm begins deep inside her, the epicenter being at the tip of Allister's driving cock. Dawn plants her feet on the bed, arching her back and pressing her hips toward Allister, as she locks her arms around his shoulders, pulling her upper body against his. A sensation like none she's ever felt before overtakes Dawn's body, and every muscle tightens to her drawn out scream.

"Oh god!"

Allister answers with a strained and barely audible, "I'm cumming!"

Dawn feels Allister's warm stream flood her depths, and his muscles stiffen as she holds him securely, clamping her pussy around his heaving cock. Allister continues to move in and out of Dawn as he cums, always pausing and pressing at the deepest point. Dawn reacts with each movement, her muscles flexing and relaxing in quick succession. They kiss frantically as their orgasms trail off, holding each other steadfastly while pausing to catch their breath.

Dawn places her hand on Allister's cheek as he pulls back from their kiss, and her eyelids flutter as she attempts to focus on his features. As the fog clears from her head she is able to see Allister's sharp blue eyes staring back at her, which brings a coy smile to her face. As they lay there staring at each other, Allister smoothly sways his hips. A sudden convulsion of Allister's cock reveals to Dawn that he is still very hard inside of her. Allister's sways become advances that grow stronger and reach deeper with each turn of his hips. Dawn rolls her head back and closes her eyes, as she begins to mirror Allister's actions.

"Yes," Dawn whimpers. "Again."

Whether that was a command, a request or an acknowledgement, Allister eagerly agrees and presses on, lunging forward with his hips, igniting Dawn's pussy with long, slow strokes. Then unexpectedly, he pulls out of her. Dawn opens her eyes to see Allister sit up and kneel between her legs. He takes hold of her hips, guiding her to roll over onto her stomach. Dawn lets out a playful squeal of surprise as she succumbs to the gentle force that Allister uses to manhandle her body, and she gives way to his direction, laying face down and pressing her forehead into the pillow. She forces her open hands against the bed and raises her hips, surrendering herself to Allister's desire.

It isn't long before Dawn feels Allister's hands on her hips, and his cock plunging deep into her pussy. She buries her face in the pillow, muffling the sounds compelled by the aggressive entry. Allister falls forward, placing his hands on the bed beside Dawn's, his back arching as his arms straighten and lift his upper body while his hips slowly press forward. Although weakened by his orgasm, Allister's advance is still powerful, and his balls flog Dawn's clit while his thighs slap her backside, as he summons the energy to continue. Dawn reaches up and pushes against the headboard, raising her hips higher and lifting her face from the pillow, allowing Allister to more clearly hear her as she entices him with playful encouragement.

"Oh my!" Dawn teases, placing her hands back down on the bed, raising herself onto all fours, her back meeting Allister's chest. She tosses her head back, turning her face to one side and placing her lips next to Allister's ear. "Are you going to cum again Allister? Cum for me."

Allister answers by lifting himself up and placing his hands back on Dawn's hips. Gripping firmly, he quickens the pace – each forward strike punctuated with grunts and groans, willing his body to respond to Dawn's wish. Dawn reacts to the steadily increasing momentum with pleasure filled purrs and further encouragement.

"Yes – cum for me – deep inside me Allister – cum."

Allister reacts with shorter, quicker strokes, each accompanied by an enthusiastic "yes" from Dawn. Then with one powerful thrust forward, Allister plants the head of his cock deep inside Dawn and holds it there. He lets out a growl, as cum surges through his flexing cock, erupting from the tip and warming the recesses of Dawn's pussy. Allister edges back until the head of his cock is all that remains inside, and then he eases forward again, sinking his full length back into place as Dawn tightens her muscles, extracting all of the cum and pleasure that Allister aptly provides.

Allister, breathing heavily, lowers his chest down onto Dawn's back, and kisses her shoulder. Dawn feels Allister's penis soften inside of her before it eventually slips out, as he rolls away, laying on his back beside her, still taking deep breaths. Dawn stretches out onto her stomach and stares at Allister with a mischievous grin, taking moderate pride in her lover's exhaustion.

"How about a shower?" Dawn suggests, rolling over and leaping from the bed. "That is exactly what I need right now," Allister smiles, watching Dawn's soft, round bottom as she struts from the room. He stares at the vacant doorway, holding onto Dawn's image in his mind, not moving until he hears running water from across the hall.

Allister enters the bathroom and discovers Dawn already in the shower, her figure visible through the translucent shower curtain. Her back is to the shower spray and her head is tilted, allowing the water to flow through her hair as her hands move over her breasts and stomach. Allister pulls back the curtain and steps into the tub at the end opposite of the shower head, and Dawn instantly welcomes him with a kiss. Then holding his shoulders, she guides him around herself and places him under the rushing water. Taking a shower puff from its hook, she snatches a bottle of body wash from one of the shelves and squirts some of the soap into her hands, kneading it into the puff to produce a slather of bubbles before presenting it to Allister.

"Wash me?" Dawn asks.

"I'd love too," Allister responds.

Taking the puff from Dawn and squeezing more bubbles from it Allister touches it to her skin. His eyes follow the puff as it smooths over her body – starting at her shoulders, then across her breasts. Dawn turns, allowing him to wash her back and her bottom, that moments earlier he had admired as she left him laying on the bed. Allister is thorough and covers every inch of Dawn's body, even lifting each of her legs to wash her thighs, calves and feet. Having coated her with suds, he steps aside to allow her to rinse off. He drops the puff and uses his hands to help remove the last of the bubbles. Rinsed clean, Dawn picks up the puff and applies more body wash.

"My turn to wash you."

She begins washing Allister, just as he had done for her, starting at his shoulders and moving down over his chest and stomach. After covering his front with an abundance of foam, she spins him around to face the water, allowing him to rinse his chest while she works on his back. Again, she starts at his broad shoulders before moving down his back and over his bum. Dawn doesn't lift Allister's legs, but instead kneels down in the tub to wash the backs of them. Then brushing away the suds, she places a kiss on his bum cheek, provoking him to look over his shoulder and smile down at her as she looks up, smiling back. She motions for him to turn around, and as he does, she runs the puff up and down his thighs.

Allister's soft penis dangles at eye level before Dawn. Try as she might to pay attention to what her hands are doing as she washes Allister's legs, her eyes are drawn to his penis. The temptation is too much for her to resist and she leans forward, lifting Allister's penis with her tongue, and taking it wholly into her mouth. She uses her tongue to explore every inch of the soft member, pressing it against the inside of her cheeks and orally massaging it deeply. Her mouth pleasantly occupied, Dawn manages a grin as she looks up at Allister, but he doesn't look back – he's staring up at the ceiling, his hands holding his head. At the same time, Dawn feels Allister's penis growing in her mouth, and she can't believe that he's getting hard again so quickly. She allows his penis to drop from her mouth before it reaches full erection, and she stands up to face him.

"Mr. Copeland!" Dawn flirts as she once more spreads suds over Allister's chest. "Are we getting hard again?"

"I can't help it," Allister blushes. "You do something to me. You're amazing. I didn't think I had it in me, really. It's never been like this before."

"You flatter me," Dawn continues, using the same playful, yet formal tone. "Whatever will I do about that?"

Dawn drops the puff and motions for Allister to face the shower head, turning his back to her. She reaches around and rubs his chest, brushing away the soap as she stands on her toes, leaning in close and whispering.

"You have the most beautiful cock I have ever seen."

Allister tilts his head back toward Dawn, listening carefully as she breathes words into his ear.

"The shape, the size, the way that you slide it in and out of my pussy. I've never had an orgasm like that in my life – thanks to you and your perfect cock."

As much as Dawn designs her words to stimulate Allister, they reflect the truth, and as she speaks them, a flame ignites within her. Dawn's kisses burn a line down Allister's back as her nails gently trace their way from his chest to his stomach. The sensation is almost euphoric for Allister, and he drifts forward slightly, hanging his head and placing his hands on the wall. Dawn's hands reach Allister's semi-erect penis as she places a kiss on his left butt cheek, and she begins to massage his growing cock delicately, with an open hand. Her other hand continues on its journey, circling his hips and spreading his legs slightly. Allister's balls hang freely between his legs, and Dawn uses her free hand, reaching from behind to cup them, giving them a graceful massage.

The water from the shower trickles down Allister's back and over his bum, and Dawn laps at the streams, licking the water off of his butt cheeks. Allister's cock swells, and he looks down at Dawn's hand as she wraps it around the shaft and begins masturbating him with an upturned grip. The massage of Allister's balls continues, and Dawn places her face between his legs, pulling the soft orbs into her mouth one at a time, giving each equal attention with her tongue.

Allister's arms begin to weaken, causing him to lean forward further, pressing his cheek against the wall as he breathes heavily. A river of water runs down between the crack of his butt, finding it's way to his balls, and Dawn's lips. She follows the stream upward, pressing deeply with her tongue, pausing for a moment at a most sensitive spot before continuing up the valley. Once at the top of Allister's bum, Dawn begins placing soft kisses on his lower back while continually pulling at his cock, and graciously manipulating his balls.

"Allister?" Dawn asks in between kisses. Allister doesn't respond, so Dawn repeats, "Allister?"

Realizing that Dawn is expecting a response, Allister forces the words out with a laugh.

"Yes – Dawn?"

Pushing aside the twinge of guilt she feels for making Allister actually respond, Dawn holds back her own devilish laughter and continues, spacing her words between the kisses that she's placing on Allister's back.

"Would you – like me – to suck – your cock?"

"Oh god!" comes Allister's immediate reply.

However, Dawn isn't quite finished taunting yet. And again, she spaces her words with kisses.

"I want – you to cum – in my mouth."

And with that, she grabs Allister's hips and steers his body around to face her, the head of his cock hovering before her lips. She looks up with a sly smile and slips her tongue out of her mouth, brushing the tip with a salacious lick.

"Oh my god, Dawn," Allister whimpers.

Dawn grabs Allister's bum with both hands, forcing her lips over his cock. She works to hold him in her mouth, but she is forced back as his stiff cock pushes against the back of her throat – the full length too much for her to handle. Unthwarted, she grips Allister's solid shaft with her hand, holding the swollen head in her mouth, playing with it with her tongue. Again, she pushes forward, taking as much of Allister into her wanting mouth. Allister raises his arms and presses his hands against the ceiling of the shower trying to keep his balance as Dawn pumps his cock with her hand and mouth. He looks down at Dawn, and she is staring straight back up at him. The desire in her eyes takes hold of him as his orgasm begins to build, watching her lick, suck and pump his cock. In an attempt to warn Dawn, Allister's mouth falls open, and he struggles to form words between heated breaths.

"I'm – cum – ing!"

The warning goes unheeded and Dawn's eyes alight with expectation as Allister continues to stare in apparent disbelief, feeling the cum race through his cock, and burst from the tip into Dawn's mouth. Her lips manage a grin as she holds the head of his exploding cock on the back of her tongue, draining it with both hands. Allister's eyes widen as the flow subsides, and he watches Dawn pull back, closing her mouth and swallowing hard, her face beaming with satisfaction. She places faint kisses along the length of Allister's shaking cock, and causes it to leap when she flicks her tongue across the sensitive tip.

The extra attention keeps Allister's cock firm, but he is unsure if he physically has anything left to give Dawn. He motions for her to stand, and when she complies he wraps his arms around her and pulls her close, kissing her deeply. It's at that moment that he decides to discover if the desire driving his mind and emotions is strong enough to drive his tiring body. He places his hands on Dawn's hips, holding her to him. Twisting his body, he presses her back against the side wall of the shower. Then cupping her bum with his hands, he lifts her off of her feet.

The water beats down on both of them as Dawn wraps her legs around Allister's waist and lowers herself down onto his waning erection. The silky lining of Dawn's pussy closes in around the tender head and shaft of Allister's cock, bringing new life to the tired muscle. Dawn is astonished by Allister's perseverance as she feels him grow inside of her, once again reclaiming it's fully aroused state. She stretches out her toes and finds the edge of the tub, while Allister uses what little strength he has left in his arms to raise and lower her, as his cock probes the depths of her pussy searching for the spot that pleases her so much.

"There!" Dawn calls out as Allister pin-points the location. "There – yes – yes!"

Allister pushes on, his muscles strained to their limit as he lifts Dawn and then lowers her back down, penetrating her deeply. Dawn wraps her arms around Allister's head and holds his face to her breasts, as she feels her orgasm beg to be released. She bites her bottom lip, trying to control the volume of her cry, but it is futile as she begins to climax.

"Oh my god – yes!"

Dawn's words echo through the small room again and again. She forces her mouth down onto Allister's shoulder, whimpering – almost crying, as her orgasm repeatedly rises then abates in waves that pummel her body. The massive release leaves Dawn's body shaking, and Allister holds her tenderly in his arms. Dawn can feel Allister's heart pounding as he pants furiously, but that isn't all she feels. She also feels the throbbing of his cock inside of her, the one part of him that doesn't seem ready to quit.

Dawn lifts herself off of Allister and lowers her feet to the floor of the tub. She plants a small kiss on his lips before sliding down his body and kneeling in front of him. Allister can only shake his head and smile, feeling he has nothing left, but too exhausted to protest. Dawn counters Allister's shaking head and smile with a nod and a smile of her own, the look in her eyes telling him that protesting won't do him any good. Allister, is not prepared for just how determined Dawn is, as she grabs his ass firmly and pulls him in. Dawn is not about to allow Allister's length or her own reflexes stop her this time, and she advances on his cock, opening her throat, taking the full length of his pulsing erection into her mouth and holding it there, surprising both Allister and herself.

"God – Dawn!"

The words fly from Allister, as he throws his head back, palming his face. He looks down at Dawn just as his cock exits her mouth, only to see her breathe deeply and drive forward again, taking him all of the way in – and again, he throws his head back as Dawn's throat closes around the head of his cock. Allister reaches behind himself, leaning back and grabbing the wall in an attempt to gain some sort of control, but Dawn is in control, and Allister can only watch helplessly as his entire cock disappears once more through her lips.

Allister's chest heaves as he struggles to catch his breath, but soon there comes a reprieve as Dawn pulls her head back, releasing his cock. Allister exhales deeply, then quickly fills his lungs again, brought on by the force of Dawn plunging him further than ever into her relaxed throat. Dawn's nose presses against Allister's stomach and her bottom lip glances his balls. She holds herself there for as long as she is able, allowing the muscles of her throat to completely relax, closing in around Allister's trembling cock. Suddenly, Allister lets out a groan, sounding like a body builder struggling to lift too much weight, and Dawn feels the stream of cum spurt from Allister's cock, into her throat.

The small amount of creamy, liquid does not compare to the powerful sensations taking over Allister's body as he orgasms yet again. The head of his cock is severely sensitive now, and he tries to pull back, but Dawn only allows him to pull halfway out, catching cum on her tongue before pushing forward again, her mouth and throat engulfing Allister's tingling cock. Allister doubles over, placing his hands on Dawn's back as she swallows head, shaft and cum. Bent over and shaking, Allister's mouth opens wide as his lips twitch, but words fail him as he grabs Dawn's head and holds on, his fingers entangled in her hair – until finally, Dawn pulls back one last time and allows Allistar to sink to the floor of the tub.

Dawn lays down beside Allister, throwing her one leg over both of his, tenderly kissing and touching his chest. Allister wraps his arms around her, closing his eyes, utterly spent. Watching as Allister's penis softens and shrinks, Dawn reaches out, carefully caressing it with her fingers.

"No more," Allister begs. "I have nothing left."

"Don't worry," Dawn laughs. "I'm just admiring."

"Dawn." Allister struggles with his words, repeating, "Dawn..."

"Allister?" Dawn interrupts. "Will you stay the night?"

"Thank you – Yes."

They stand in the tub, rinsing off one more time before Dawn shuts off the water. Dawn takes a towel from the rack and hands it to Allister before grabbing one for herself. They dry off and leave the bathroom, pausing to pet Cleo, who has been waiting patiently in the hallway. They are both exhausted as they enter the bedroom, and stroll directly to the bed. Turning down the covers, they lay down beside each other and drag a sheet up and over, covering their bodies. Dawn stares up at the ceiling as the days events run through her mind, and she contemplates aloud.

"I think that was the most exhausting day I've ever had."

"Ever?" Allister asks.

"I'm pretty sure. I don't know if I can move another inch."

"But was it a good day?"

"It was an excellent day – especially the ending."

Allister smiles, still reeling from the multiple endings. "Well it was definitely the most amazing day of my life."

Dawn smiles.

After one final kiss goodnight Allister closes his eyes, and Dawn switches off the lamp that sits atop the night stand.

12:00 AM

"Allister?"
"Yes, Dawn?"
"Could I get a ride into work in the morning?"

THE END

.

www.ingramcontent.com/pod-product-compliance
Lightning Source LLC
Chambersburg PA
CBHW060420260626
47161CB00005B/1714